▶ Swift, Joyce, and the Flight from Home

DOI: 10.1057/9781137399823.0001

Also by G. Douglas Atkins

THE FAITH OF JOHN DRYDEN: Change and Continuity

READING DECONSTRUCTION/DECONSTRUCTIVE READING

WRITING AND READING DIFFERENTLY: Deconstruction and the Teaching of Composition and Literature (*co-edited with Michael L. Johnson*)

QUESTS OF DIFFERENCE: Reading Pope's Poems

SHAKESPEARE AND DECONSTRUCTION (*co-edited with David M. Bergeron*)

CONTEMPORARY LITERARY THEORY (*co-edited with Laura Morrow*)

GEOFFREY HARTMAN: Criticism as Answerable Style

ESTRANGING THE FAMILIAR: Toward a Revitalized Critical Writing

TRACING THE ESSAY: Through Experience to Truth

READING ESSAYS: An Invitation

ON THE FAMILIAR ESSAY: Challenging Academic Orthodoxies

LITERARY PATHS TO RELIGIOUS UNDERSTANDING: Essays on Dryden, Pope, Keats, George Eliot, Joyce, T.S. Eliot, and E.B. White

T.S. ELIOT AND THE ESSAY: From *The Sacred Wood* to *Four Quartets*

READING T.S. ELIOT: *Four Quartets* and the Journey toward Understanding

E.B. WHITE: The Essayist as First-Class Writer

T.S. ELIOT MATERIALIZED: Literal Meaning and Embodied Truth

SWIFT'S SATIRES ON MODERNISM: Battlegrounds of Reading and Writing

ALEXANDER POPE'S CATHOLIC VISION: "Slave to no sect"

T.S. ELIOT AND THE FAILURE TO CONNECT: Satire and Modern Misunderstandings

T.S. ELIOT, LANCELOT ANDREWES, AND THE WORD: Intersections of Literature and Christianity

DOI: 10.1057/9781137399823.0001

palgrave▶**pivot**

Swift, Joyce, and the Flight from Home: Quests of Transcendence and the Sin of Separation

G. Douglas Atkins

▶

palgrave
macmillan

DOI: 10.1057/9781137399823.0001

SWIFT, JOYCE, AND THE FLIGHT FROM HOME
Copyright © G. Douglas Atkins, 2014.

First published in 2014 by
PALGRAVE MACMILLAN®
in the United States—a division of St. Martin's Press LLC,
175 Fifth Avenue, New York, NY 10010.

Where this book is distributed in the UK, Europe and the rest of the world,
this is by Palgrave Macmillan, a division of Macmillan Publishers Limited,
registered in England, company number 785998, of Houndmills,
Basingstoke, Hampshire RG21 6XS.

Palgrave Macmillan is the global academic imprint of the above companies
and has companies and representatives throughout the world.

Palgrave® and Macmillan® are registered trademarks in the United States,
the United Kingdom, Europe and other countries.

ISBN: 978-1-137-39983-0 EPUB
ISBN: 978-1-137-39982-3 PDF
ISBN: 978-1-137-39981-6 Hardback

Library of Congress Cataloging-in-Publication Data is available from
the Library of Congress.

A catalogue record of the book is available from the British Library.

First edition: 2014

www.palgrave.com/pivot

DOI: 10.1057/9781137399823

▶ *To students in my Freshman Honors courses 1969–2012, University of Kansas*

DOI: 10.1057/9781137399823.0001

Contents

DOI: 10.1057/9781137399823.0001

Preface

Although this volume represents something of a continuation of my recent book on Swift and modernism, in which I focused on the treatment of reading (and writing) in *A Tale of a Tub*, its "concorde" with my explorations of T.S. Eliot will be every bit as apparent. I have recently written of *The Waste Land* as satire, and I continue to find Eliot's understanding of Incarnation fundamental to literature and living, alike. Eliot edited a selection of "Joyce's prose" for Faber and Faber and much admired, among other things, his use of the "mythical method" by which disparate time periods are brought together in measurement of one another, but he said little about Swift (or Pope, either) while devoting considerable attention and effort to other figures of the Restoration and eighteenth century, most notably Dryden and Johnson. I offer my commentary here as no attempt to right a wrong or to speak for Old Possum, although the point of view readily apparent and functional shares a great deal with Eliot's Anglo-Catholic Christianity and his classicism (if not also with his "royalism"). Point of view is just the issue, and I offer this little book as *my* essay to get right two critical writers' insights concerning precisely the necessity of bringing together, comparing, and "amalgamating disparate experience." "Suffer us not to be separated," says *Ash-Wednesday: Six Poems* at the close, and *Four Quartets* masterfully reveals our penchant for (only) *half*-understanding.

A word or two may not be amiss concerning my own way of reading and writing about reading. As I explain in Chapter 1, reading always involves (at least) two, and I

DOI: 10.1057/9781137399823.0002

regard it as an act consisting of the intersection of text and reader. That means my point of view is very much evident, although it does not—I pray—dominate. Point of view differs from theory, as day from night. Today, students are often taught to approach a literary text from a variety of theories, Lacanian, for example, deconstructive, Marxist, queer, postcolonial, the object being to teach them relativism: one is as good as another, there being no "paradigm" in this "seriality" (as Derrida put it). I have, in my benighted past, applied deconstructive theory to Pope's poems—will-fully "imposed" it upon them, really. Point of view, differently, is "Behovely," that is, unavoidable. But it need not be determinative, nor does it exist as one among many choices. The burden is on the reader to choose; value judgments, too, are unavoidable, and we need to return to this fundamental human fact and begin (again) to teach our students how to make good judgments. You could do much worse than to start with (that is, from) Eliot.

Comparison is tricky business. It smacks, at least to many, of relativism. To others perhaps, it appears as much ado about nothing. Some maintain, indeed, that comparison of, say, Swift and Joyce, offers little beyond what close attention to each, apart and separately, reveals. I maintain, however, that comparison does more, enabling our reading in ways unavailable to "unitary" efforts. Revealing similarities and differences alike, comparison brings to the fore issues, perspectives, and treatments that we might otherwise miss or minimize; it sharpens our awareness of issues, perspectives, and treatments; and it helps to confirm some readings while disabusing us of others. In the case of *Gulliver's Travels* and *A Portrait of the Artist as a Young Man*, both works blessed and damned alike by virtually opposite "hard" and "soft" interpretations of their protagonists, comparison allows, as Eliot said, for "measurement," enabling critical assessment of various sorts. You know Gulliver better by juxtaposing him with Stephen, Stephen by juxtaposition with Gulliver, or so I maintain.

What is new about my readings of the two books is both the comparison that enables critical measurement and the Incarnational point of view from and within which I write, a position that is itself heavily dependent upon comparison and that is, in fact, made of the association that stands counter to such separation as comes between entities, obviating positive relations. I am contending, moreover, that the Incarnational point of view from and within which I write is that shared by Swift, Anglican churchman, and Joyce, putative apostate of the Roman Church.

DOI: 10.1057/9781137399823.0002

In other words, I seek to bring out what is there, *in* these great texts. And *that*, I further maintain, has to do with a timeless and universal pattern. A person—perhaps Homer, for example, centuries before Christ—may be Incarnational (whether consciously or not) without subscribing to Christian dogma. It is a matter, as Eliot's Ariel Poem *Triumphal March* reveals, not of perception but of understanding (itself another name of the Second Person of the Christian Trinity).

Another way of putting the same thing: This book may be read as a comparison of my own point of view with that of Swift and that of Joyce. Just as I compare the two writers, so my point of view stands in measurement both of and by the great works here read. It is, then, a matter of text and reader, with the ultimate goal of text—what Swift and Joyce actually *say*—intersecting with me and my reading of them.

As to Swift and Joyce, the presence of Incarnational pattern in Swift can hardly surprise, given his professional and spiritual commitment to the Church of Ireland. Joyce is another matter altogether. While I believe him acutely aware of pattern, and indeed of the character of Incarnational pattern (manifest, for example, in the subtle and shrewd rhetorical use of Stephen's *memory* of "darkness" falling from the air juxtaposed with the *reality* that "Brightness falls from the air"), I think it may count more—to the point of confirming my critical argument—if he were not so aware. That is to say, a non-Christian, even an anti-Christian, lives and works in a world governed by Incarnational pattern, no matter his or her intentions or the content or extent of his awareness.

Furthermore I offer here *commentary*, which I understand as a quite precise critical term. By the word, I mean, among other things, analysis that proceeds from the close reading of specific passages, adduced as (admittedly frequent and often lengthy) quotations. These quotations are not, as Eliot says they are not in Lancelot Andrewes, "decoration or irrelevance, but the matter in which [I express] what [I want] to say"; the thoughts are made my own, "and the constructive force, the fire that fuses them" is my own. I find repeatedly that copying out the words of the text under consideration results in the closest reading and makes available, often at least, understanding and insight that seem not otherwise available. The "commentary" that I then provide is not, despite a certain likeness, equivalent to annotation, for my comments appear in the sub-form of a narrative within the overall form of the essay. I suggest "commentary" as a viable and preferable mode of so-called critical discourse, too little practiced today.

DOI: 10.1057/9781137399823.0002

In defining "commentary" as I do, and claiming to write it here, I do not intend to suggest that my efforts—my *essais*—are concerned only or even primarily with parts, to the neglect of the whole (text). Commenting on a quoted passage may represent writing in the present moment, but if so, there is always also the past moment(s) in which the whole is apprehended in, through, and by means of the various parts, whose particular contributions and relation are inseparable from a sense, however varying, of the whole. The hermeneutical circle, so-called, is, I reckon, itself related to those instances of "impossible union" that I claim as deriving ultimately from the paradigmatic instance of that union, which Eliot names in *Four Quartets* "Incarnation."

A word or two may also be in order concerning politics, not just because such is practically obligatory these days but lest there be misunderstanding. Although, as usual, I do not write from an overtly political stance, nor engage in directly political issues, my point of view, quite different from Stephen Dedalus's aestheticism, by no means lacks political implications. Like Eliot, who made *The Sacred Wood* the first—necessary—stop on the way to doing cultural, social, and political commentary, I believe that you begin with reading texts, although you hardly rest content there. My own political point of view—essentially Tory, in the eighteenth-century sense of criticizing every position—may very well be just about the only rebellious form around nowadays, challenging the smug smog and *1984* gray stench of literary theory's political orthodoxy.

My longest-standing debts are to *magister*: Vincent Miller, at Wofford College, who taught me to read and then introduced me to Eliot and Joyce, and Irvin Ehrenpreis, at the University of Virginia, who showed me how to love the eighteenth century and to bring scholarship to bear on responsible reading. That I have not made a better book is none at all of their doing. Without their instruction, their advice, and their support, I would not have tried—and Eliot said, "For us, there is only the trying. The rest is not our business."

I am pleased to record here my debts to the many hundreds of University of Kansas students who, over forty-some years, passed through my English Honors course in the Ancients, Moderns, and Modernists, where I introduced them to *Gulliver's Travels* in unexpurgated form and tried to get them to see how they are implicated if persisting in thinking

DOI: 10.1057/9781137399823.0002

Stephen Dedalus is a hero to be admired and perhaps followed. I never ceased to learn, not least from those who disagreed with me.

I take pleasure also in acknowledging my continuing huge debt to my lovely wife Rebecca, who frees me from so many mundane tasks so that I can squirrel away in my man-cave and do what I find so rewarding, realizing my vocation; to our "kids" Leslie and Christopher, their spouses Craig and Sharon, and their kids Kate and Oliver, of each and every one of whom I am so proud and so grateful; and finally, with great sadness, to our remarkable and loving Millie, whom we lost as I was completing this little book but who gave us so very much delight, daily, hourly affirming life's newness and joy.

In addition, I am honored to record once again my gratitude and debt to Brigitte Shull of Palgrave Macmillan, New York.

Writing this book brought me great pleasure, more perhaps than from writing any other. The reason may have to do with the decidedly essayistic feel here. I can only hope that, whatever that case may be, the made-thing will give you, gentle reader, a measure of such pleasure.

DOI: 10.1057/9781137399823.0002

His throat ached with a desire to cry aloud, the cry
of a hawk or eagle on high, to cry piercingly of his
deliverance to the winds. This was the call of life to
his soul not the dull gross voice of the world of duties
and despair, not the inhuman voice that had called him
to the pale service of the altar. An instant of wild flight
had delivered him and the cry of triumph which his lips
withheld cleft his brain.

—James Joyce, *A Portrait of the Artist as a Young Man*

The wives and daughters lament their confinement to the
island, although I think it the most delicious spot of ground
in the world.

—Jonathan Swift, *Gulliver's Travels*

DOI: 10.1057/9781137399823.0002

1
Satire, Reading, and Forms of Separation and Union

Abstract: *Swift's complex satire* A Tale of a Tub *(1704) treats of both writing and reading, responding to the rise of the personal essay and pretending to be about nothing, and at the same time dramatically analyzing both the will-fulness of readers and the will-ingness of texts. It thus has much to teach us about reading, which always involves at least two, both a reader and the text. Reading appears, in fact, as a triune activity, consisting of text, reader and reading, and response (or action, beyond the act of reading). Swift's great satire also shows us something important about bringing-together, rather than separating (for example, reason and imagination).*

Atkins, G. Douglas. *Swift, Joyce, and the Flight from Home: Quests of Transcendence and the Sin of Separation.* New York: Palgrave Macmillan, 2014.
DOI: 10.1057/9781137399823.0003.

> It were much to be wished, and I do here humbly propose for an experiment, that every prince in Christendom will take seven of the deepest scholars in his dominions, and shut them up close for seven years in seven chambers, with a command to write seven ample commentaries on this comprehensive discourse. I shall venture to affirm, that whatever difference may be found in their several conjectures, they will be all, without the least distortion, manifestly deducible from the text.
>
> Jonathan Swift, *A Tale of a Tub*

Swift's first great satire, *A Tale of a Tub,* puts critic and reader alike on the spot. Published in 1704, 22 years before *Travels into Several Remote Nations of the World,* familiarly known as *Gulliver's Travels,* this perplexing, often nearly maddening satire treats the will-fulness of readers in face of the willing nature of texts; the result is a bewildering series of chapters of religious allegory alternating (generally) with so-called digressions on critics and criticism that for many readers defies their best attempts at comprehension, let alone mastery. The *Tale's* (modern) self-reflexiveness draws the reader in, implicating him or her in the critique of textual manipulation and perversion. The book appears to hang together by the merest thread.

Critics come in for much of the opprobrium: both their will-ful misuse of texts and their writing in a form owing much to the personal essay that, ultimately, amounts to what the hack-narrator shamelessly embraces as "writ[ing] upon *Nothing*."[1] "Invention" names the problem, as moderns forsake established forms and traditions; it is a sort of pernicious "enthusiasm":

> when a man's fancy gets astride on his reason, when imagination is at cuffs with the senses, and common understanding, as well as common sense, is kicked out of doors, the first proselyte he makes is himself; and when that is once compassed, the difficulty is not so great in bringing over others; a strong delusion always operating from without as vigorously as from within.[2]

Thus occur, says the satire, all the revolutions that have disastrously occurred in government, philosophy, and religion. As well as in literary forms and critical theory, one might add.

Implicit in the lengthy quotation above is the problem, unbeknownst to the (satirized) narrator, of course: imagination is not so much the

DOI: 10.1057/9781137399823.0003

matter as its separation from reason, from the senses, from "common understanding." When the latter is "kicked out of doors," then imagination reigns without the guidance that Swift's friend Alexander Pope insisted is necessary. Contrary, therefore, to the frequent assumption, Swift does not posit an either/or between reason or the senses and imagination; instead, and desirably, they come together, or not.

The structure revealed above, an essential both/and rather than either/or, is apparent in satire itself, albeit in complex fashion. First of all, satire functions—and can only succeed—when both "thesis" and "antithesis" are available to a reader: that is, the satirist's object(s) of opprobrium and his answer, alternative, or solution. If no such "positive" appears to the "negative" that occupies the center and brunt of attention, the reader flounders, as happened in the instance of Swift's contemporary Daniel Defoe and his *Shortest Way with Dissenters*, which offers no evident place to stand and render judgment and reproach. Defoe, we might say, fails to establish or at least to make sufficiently clear to a responsible reader a "still point" that governs and directs the "movement" that the author wants to denigrate.

Movement, then, needs pattern, and pattern emerges out of and from movement; as Eliot puts it in "Burnt Norton," first of *Four Quartets*, "Only by the form, the pattern,/ Can words or music reach/ The stillness"; at the same time, he adds, "The detail of the pattern is movement."[3] In a rather different though related way, satirical "antithesis" requires a "thesis," just as the latter does the former (even if, in satire, opposition is set up between "them" and "us"). Although engaged in *opposing*, that is, often vituperative, angry, and even savage in that opposition, the writer, no doubt unwillingly at times, reveals through his or her mode or form—that of satire—that positive and negative are locked in ineluctable and structurally definable relation: one may exist without the other, but cannot function properly or expect to succeed. It is a rather humbling recognition.

Reading, as it happens, participates in the same essential structure. Consider the "actors" involved in every instance of the "drama":

Text
Reader

Swift's great modern biographer, Irvin Ehrenpreis, has made the point simply but eloquently, a point that, for some reason, we have grave and persistent trouble grasping and accepting:

[A]ll literary works, whether by Swift or anyone else, depend for their life on a relationship between author and audience. What the reader may see

DOI: 10.1057/9781137399823.0003

does not exist in the work unless it can be imputed to the author (known or unknown) in his capacity as artist. Conversely, what the author may intend has no literary reality unless it can be discovered in his work by a proper reader. *Each man exists in art only as an object for the other's contemplation,* defined by those aspects of himself which can be interested or embodied in the public, literary terms of the work as read or heard. (Italics added)[4]

The point of view of Ehrenpreis's Virginia colleague E.D. Hirsch, Jr., may be heard in these words.[5] Although I have some doubts about the above remarks (e.g., the notion of a "proper" reader), I believe Ehrenpreis's statement concerning the binary character of the act of reading is suggestive and valuable, perhaps even more than he realized, especially in the words that I have italicized. The statement points to the same ineluctable both/and relation noticed above in satire.

As important as the above realizations are regarding reading, they by no means tell the whole story. Reading is more complicated, a more complex act, than we have yet glimpsed. We may, in fact, supplement the binary character of reading in the following manner, surely a more nearly complete rendering of the essential and intricate act:

Text
Reader/ Reading
(Later) response, or Action

I have again preferred "Text" to "Author," being more uncomfortable with Hirsch's insistence on the primacy of authorial intention than Ehrenpreis. I have, furthermore, made the act of reading triune, rather than binary, in order to account for the likelihood that, as Geoffrey Hartman has put it, the difference that reading makes is, "most generally, writing"[6] as well as for the very real possibility that the affected reader engages in activity inspired or prompted by his reading that takes place after the book, poem, novel, or essay is put down. Finally, in this triune structure, I have divided the second part in two, effectively turning three into four.

Another way of saying it, influenced by Hartman's account of reading in relation to William Butler Yeats's great poem "Leda and the Swan," itself a sort of allegory of reading:[7] The text visits, intersects with, and impregnates its respondent, who, as *receiver*, is in the position of possibly *conceiving* a "new birth" that, as it were, acts beyond the text. The reader must, in this formulation, be open and responsive to, in other words, fertile and ready for, insemination. But two things quickly expand into more. The reader does not function as such apart from the act of

DOI: 10.1057/9781137399823.0003

reading, which, likewise, does not exist without a reader; reader and reading cannot, then, be separated.

As well, in coming together, reader and text (obviously) intersecting, they may not be said to lose their identities, or to become absorbed in and by the other. There is, to put it otherwise, no transcendence of either reader or text. There is, instead, an "association," a "concorde" (to use Eliot's words), apparent and functional in this "daunsinge." Reader is no more in charge, at this point, this "intersection," than text is—the problems of will-fulness that Swift emphasized in *A Tale of a Tub* amicably resolved. Thus formulated, it sounds simple. It is, of course, far from being so.

Typically, we *half*-understand, privileging either text (or author) or reader. In literary studies, the result has been the establishment of rival camps of (Hirschian) intentionalists and reader-response critics (ranging from Stanley Fish to Wolfgang Iser and even some structuralists and poststructuralists). We humans appear to gravitate towards either/or alternatives and solutions, avoiding the complex and intricate—especially the *tensional*—whenever and wherever possible and conceivable. Insisting that texts speak, and bear authority, is tantamount to placing responsibility on the reader-receiver for trying to understand what is actually being said to him or her (complete assurance never being quite possible, no matter the effort). Insisting, at the same time, that the reader comes to the act as no blank slate or *tabula rasa* but as a fully functional human being, made of flesh and blood, with desires, experience, and will, a creature of reason and imagination, of body and soul, of sense and sensibility (as well as pride and prejudice, I dare add), means the burden of response is great, indeed. He or she needs taste and judgment, which must be developed over time and invoked in every attempt to read (and respond to) what the text is offering, its gift.

In the quotation from Swift's *A Tale of a Tub* that I have adduced as my epigraph above, the word "commentary" appears twice, referring to an approach to literary criticism, absent so many negatives, that stems from the medieval tradition treating sacred and secular texts alike that includes Dante, Petrarch, and Boccaccio. The word itself suggests, not a relativism, but the presence of the commentator often obscured in the efforts known as, if not apparent in our familiar term, "criticism." More important, the idea of "commentary," as distinguished from "criticism," seems favorably situated for the form of the *essay*, in which the speaking voice always plays a critical—arguably *the* critical—role.

DOI: 10.1057/9781137399823.0003

When, in *A Tale of a Tub*, Swift holds up for critique the (new) form inaugurated a hundred years before in France by Michel de Montaigne, and subsequently brought to England by Sir Francis Bacon, a Modern lambasted in the *Tale*'s companion-piece *The Battle of the Books*, he has in mind the personal sort, which privileges the notion of "personality" that Eliot too found so repellent and dangerous. It is always *excess* that the satirist opposes (it is also the means of his or her opposition). Thus he would refine or purify the new tradition, not purge all vestiges of it—in line with Eliot's crucial distinction between Christian and pagan notions: after all, as *Four Quartets* affirms, quoting the medieval Dame Julian of Norwich, "Sin is Behovely." As such, it can never be eliminated or transcended.

Notes

1   Jonathan Swift, *A Tale of a Tub*, in *"Gulliver's Travels" and Other Writings*, ed. Louis A. Landa (Boston, MA: Riverside-Houghton Mifflin, 1960), 352.
2   Ibid., 331–32.
3   T.S. Eliot, *Four Quartets* (New York: Harcourt, Brace, 1943).
4   Irvin Ehrenpreis, *Swift: The Man, His Works, and the Age* (Vol. 2, *Dr. Swift* [Cambridge, MA: Harvard UP, 1967], 278–79).
5   See, esp., E.D. Hirsch, *Validity in Interpretation* (New Haven, CT: Yale UP, 1967).
6   Geoffrey H. Hartman, *Criticism in the Wilderness: The Study of Literature Today* (New Haven, CT: Yale UP, 1980), 19.
7   Ibid., 21–25.

DOI: 10.1057/9781137399823.0003

2
The Gift Half Understood

Abstract: *The trouble is considerable that accompanies the structure we call reading, itself always a matter of both reader and text. It is the same as with other dualities: we get it only half-right, sacrificing, in this case, either text or reader at the expense of the other. Separation of parts of an essential whole names the issue. Eliot treats it in* Four Quartets *as he dramatizes "The complete consort dancing together," each partner supporting the other, forming an "impossible union," a "necessarye coniunction," and, in the case of writing, a community of words that becomes communion. This revealed pattern places special responsibility on comparison and requires a way of reading essentially comparative in nature.*

Atkins, G. Douglas. *Swift, Joyce, and the Flight from Home: Quests of Transcendence and the Sin of Separation.* New York: Palgrave Macmillan, 2014. DOI: 10.1057/9781137399823.0004.

> It is a judgment, a comparison, in which two
> things are measured by each other.
>
> T.S. Eliot, "Tradition and the Individual Talent," *The Sacred Wood*

The structure that we examined in Chapter 1 Eliot defines in his great essay-poem *Four Quartets* (1943) as "impossible union."[1] The paradigmatic instance of such union is Incarnation, the paradigmatic instance of that being *the* Incarnation (of God in human form, in the Person of Jesus the Christ). Eliot says, though, that, typically, we grasp but half of that whole: "The hint half guessed, the gift half understood, is Incarnation."

In a striking scene earlier in the poem, set in East Coker, the poet's ancestral home, Eliot describes rustics dancing around a bonfire on a summer's eve. The orthography suggests that the time is Elizabethan, his intellectual and spiritual home as is readily apparent from his various critical writings. The depiction in "East Coker" is highly charged. "I am here," Eliot writes, concluding this, the first section of the second poem in *Four Quartets*, "Or there, or elsewhere. In my beginning."

The description pointedly rhymes with the account in "The Dry Salvages," the third poem in *Four Quartets*, of Incarnation (and thus with the account of writing in the final section of "Little Gidding," the last poem). It participates, in fact, in the pattern that Incarnation names. Incarnation is Itself a pattern, of which the scene in question is an instance.

Eliot sets it up in an "open field," on a "summer midnight," warning that "you can hear the music" "If you do not come too close, if you do not come too close." ("Comparison and analysis"[2] are one thing, dissection quite another, made up of too close an examination, a certain distance being always necessary, rather than absorption or immersion.) The "daunsinge" consists of "The association of man and woman," which "signif[ies] matrimonie," said to be a "dignified and commodious sacrament." "Couples dancing"—"Two and two"—both serves as, and makes clear, "necessarye coniunction" as they hold "eche other by the hand or the arm / Which betokeneth concorde." These are perfectly ordinary folk, rustics in fact, going round and round the fire, leaping, taking pleasure and delight, joining "in circles, / Rustically solemn or in rustic laughter"—"or" thus becomes "both." Unlike those moderns in *The Waste Land*, their virtual opposites, these country people engage in "mirth," people now long since "under earth / Nourishing the corn." They "keep" time, keep "rhythm in their dancing" as they do "in their living in the living seasons." They are not disconnected, from each other, the earth that bore them and to which they return, or the seasons; they are not separated but joined, in "concorde."

When, in the last verses of the paragraph, Eliot refers to sexual intercourse, he sets off both a rhyme and an(other) entailed difference from *The Waste Land*: "The time of the coupling of man and woman / And that of beasts. Feet rising and falling. / Eating and drinking. Dung and death." The lines make me think, as well, of *Gulliver's Travels* (with its alleged "excremental vision").[3] Eliot links man, woman, and "beasts," and his word "coupling" accentuates the relation, but without reducing or demeaning the human act; indeed, here sex appears, despite the appearance, less animalistic than in *The Waste Land*, where men and women recognize no apparent relation at all to the lower animals or keep time or rhythm with the seasons (which, in fact, they pervert and subvert in taking winter as a source of warmth, spring as nuisance, "stirring dull roots" and perhaps bringing about fruition that *they* may well choose to abort).

It bears repeating that the scene in "East Coker" is quite ordinary, the people as plain and simple as the dancing in which they engage and that brings them pleasure (and perhaps meaning, even if be not intellectualized). That this ordinary occurrence, infinitely repeatable and endlessly enjoyable and rewarding, participates in the structure that we have been observing, in the pattern that Eliot defines as Incarnation, is just the point. The representation is *attended* by that recognition, attributable to the poet but requiring the reader to activate and energize it; in parallel fashion, *what* is represented is not merely this one instance of dancing, association, and "concorde" but an "attendance" via participation in that timeless, universal pattern. In this moment, in Elizabethan England, in the countryside, on a summer midnight, *as in* and *because of* the Incarnation of the Logos in human flesh, "the intersection of the timeless moment / Is England and nowhere. Never and always" ("Little Gidding"). Eliot offers in the last of *Four Quartets* a passage that itself represents an "intersection" of the night in Bethlehem, the visit in 1642 of King Charles I to the thriving Anglican community at Little Gidding (subsequently destroyed by Cromwellian hordes), and a contemporary's coming to visit the ruins ("where prayer has been valid"), concluding, "this is the nearest, in place and time, / Now and in England."

An ascetic, thus separated from "the world" and so given to *half*-truth (and "falsehood"), the voice speaking at the opening of *Ash-Wednesday*:

DOI: 10.1057/9781137399823.0004

Six Poems has it all wrong. He believes, and asserts, that time, like place, "is always" only that, "And what is actual is actual only for one time / And only for one place."[4] *The Waste Land* already knew enough to doubt any such, the famous opening lines requiring that the reader bring to bear on them their "*semblable*," that is, the echoing and rhyming lines opening Chaucer's medieval poem *The Canterbury Tales.* The "mythical method" that Eliot praised Joyce for employing in *Ulysses* gives the lie to the voices of separation and "oneness."[5]

More than once, I have used the word "attended" to describe this situation of intersection, where one time and one place rhyme with another time and another place. The idea and the word itself I take from Eliot, in the fifth section of "The Dry Salvages," leading up to the definition of Incarnation: "For most of us there is only the unattended / Moment, the moment in and out of time." With the Incarnation, every moment became "attended," that is, burning with meaning. Meaning no longer resides above and beyond "the world," in some nether land of forms and the ideal; it has, that is to say, become "immanent" in our world, no longer simply "transcendent" to it. Meaning is here and now. As a result, each moment, like every place, is intersected by the eternal, the extra-ordinary now functioning within the ordinary. Every moment is, then, in this sense, epiphantic. Rather than, as Jacques Derrida claimed, "seriality without paradigm,"[6] each and every point in a series, all series, is, as it were, equally special and paradigmatic. We may, therefore, appreciate the rustic Elizabethans dancing around a bonfire on a summer's midnight for what the scene is: a fully special, burningly meaningful instance of Incarnation, than which none in time is more (or less) important.

Of late, I have written often of Incarnation, particularly Eliot's (possibly unorthodox) understanding of it. More than once, reviewers of my recent books have found my accounts unclear. Most recently, in a review of my book *T.S. Eliot and the Essay: From "The Sacred Wood" to "Four Quartets,"* Martin Lockerd has described my definition as "loose." He goes on to charge that "What Atkins means by 'incarnation' remains too vague to summarize with any surety."[7] Without, I hope, appearing merely defensive, I answer that the reviewer's difficulty with my explanations stems from his own failure to capitalize the word, as above. I am tempted to allege as well a basic failure to comprehend the central Christian dogma in and of itself, apart from Eliot's representation of it or my interpretation of it. I am reminded, though, of my own students' incapacities before the term,

DOI: 10.1057/9781137399823.0004

around which they have often merely floundered (hardly "daunsinge" in "concorde"). To be sure, these days too few students possess even the barest knowledge of Christian dogma and doctrine.

Something more may be at work in our difficulties in understanding Incarnation, and Eliot noticed, and emphasized, it in *Four Quartets*. The very idea of Incarnation, he said, is difficult to grasp. In fact, just prior to offering the notion of the "attended" moment—rendered with appropriate indirectness via its "opposite"—which itself precedes the defining of Incarnation, Eliot approaches the critical matter with a stab at saying what It is, all without the merest mention of the word itself. He writes: "But to apprehend / The point of intersection of the timeless / With time is an occupation for the saint," not an "occupation," really, "but something given / And taken, in a lifetime's death in love, / Ardor and selflessness and self-surrender." "For most of us," Eliot goes on to say, lacking a grasp on Incarnation and being no saints, there appears no intersecting of the timeless with time. Locked in time, we seek meaning outside time, perhaps in a world of Platonic forms. As Eliot says, for us, "there is only the unattended / Moment, the moment in and out of time."

We find "hints" and make "guesses," but they do little to enhance or even to enable our understanding: "the rest / Is prayer, observance, discipline, thought and action." And these are all hard, demanding—and still offer no assurance of success. We are, all too frequently at best, left with half-understanding.

In *Four Quartets*, Eliot keeps trying to *say it right*: not only to get it right but to say it so that we (finally) understand. Thus his acknowledged repetitions, alongside his repeated questions: "You say I am repeating / Something I have said before. I shall say it again. / Shall I say it again?" Words point to the problem: they are susceptible, prone to just the sort of abuse, misuse, and perversion that Swift exposed in *A Tale of a Tub*. Words are "attacked by voices of temptation," and there are always "Shrieking voices / Scolding, mocking, or merely chattering," but in any case always "assail[ing] them." Truth to tell, words themselves contribute in a major way to our difficulty in grasping such matters as Incarnation, for they "strain, / Crack and sometimes break, under the burden, / Under the tension, slip, slide, perish, / Decay with imprecision"; they simply "will not stay in place, / Will not stay still" (thus requiring that "association," and consequent overcoming of isolation and separation, that "complete consort dancing together," where "every word is at home, / Taking its place to support the others," with which *Four Quartets* draws to a close).

DOI: 10.1057/9781137399823.0004

No wonder if we fail to understand, or merely give up trying. For an instance of getting it *half*-right, take, surprisingly enough, G.K. Chesterton in an early essay "A Piece of Chalk." Chesterton went on, of course, to become a major apologist for Roman Catholicism, and Incarnational Christianity, but in this essay he commits the "falsehood" that Eliot exposes, the error partially disguised by the eloquence of the essayist's prose:

> Do not, for heaven's sake, imagine I was going to sketch from Nature. I was going to draw devils and seraphim, and blind old gods that men worshipped before the dawn of right, and saints in robes of angry crimson, and seas of strange green, and all the sacred or monstrous symbols that look so well in bright colours on brown paper. They are much better worth drawing than Nature; also they are much easier to draw. When a cow came slouching by in the field next to me, a mere artist might have drawn it; but I always get wrong in the hind legs of quadrupeds. So I drew the soul of the cow; which I saw there plainly walking before me in the sunlight; and the soul was all purple and silver, and had seven horns and the mystery that belongs to all the beasts.[8]

For an Incarnational treatment of a parallel situation, take Robert Browning's dramatic monologue "Fra Lippo Lippi," where the movement, contrariwise, is from outer to inner, the former the necessary means to the latter.

Still, the essential structure is ubiquitous, although often unrecognized. Years before Eliot's formal embrace of Anglo-Catholic Christianity in 1927, that structure appears and functions in *The Sacred Wood* (1920). The subject is (for Eliot) reviled Romanticism, the issue that of "way":

> …the only cure for Romanticism is to analyse it. What is permanent and good in Romanticism is curiosity, a curiosity which recognizes that any life, if accurately and profoundly penetrated, is interesting and always strange. Romanticism is a short cut to the strangeness without the reality, and it leads its disciples only back upon themselves.[9]

In the passage I quoted from Chesterton too, the Incarnational issue is "way," there, specifically, the means (if any) of reaching the soul.

Incarnation is, then, more than the intersection of the timeless with time or the "impossible union" of binary oppositions. It also is Way ("I am the Way," said Jesus); it is, that is to say, means as well as end. Eliot registers Incarnation as Way in "East Coker" in striking verses that repeat "way," prescribing one without ecstasy and involving paradox

DOI: 10.1057/9781137399823.0004

and contradiction. Such verses cast serious doubt upon the famous Heraclitean epigraph to "Burnt Norton": despite the Greek's authority and our familiar understanding, the way up is *not* the way down; rather, the way up is *in, through, and by means of* the way down.

The structure is Incarnational, revealed paradigmatically in the Person of Jesus Christ, who is our means of proceeding to(ward) God, there being, *pace* Stephen Dedalus, no direct route to Him. What emerges, then, is the both / and-ness of Both / And-ness: Incarnation is both means or instrument of truth *and* truth itself. In the terms of *Four Quartets*, Incarnation is both a pattern of movement and the means by which that pattern comes into being.

Reading Eliot's poems with the scrupulous attention to words that he displays in writing them, we observe that he prays in *Ash-Wednesday: Six Poems* to "Teach us to care and not to care" and, in the same vein in *Four Quartets*, that he says that "Time the destroyer is time the pre-server." There is, we further observe, a subtle but real difference in the later poem when he also writes, "Only through time time is conquered." These are related yet distinguishable aspects or shades of the meaning of Incarnation, the structure or pattern of which *the* Incarnation is—to repeat—the paradigmatic instance in human history.

One might say that with the revolution—there is no other word for it—wrought by the Incarnation a new way of knowing emerges from the shadows. Eliot embraces it, and practices it everywhere he engages in literary commentary: in *The Sacred Wood*, he says that the "tools" of criticism are two: "comparison and analysis." And in "Tradition and the Individual Talent," the best-known and most influential of the essays included in that first collection, he elaborates, briefly, in referring to "a judgment, a comparison, in which two things are measured by each other" (including the two "things" noted in his title).[10] Swift, as it happens, says something quite similar early in the second book of *Gulliver's Travels*, which pointedly juxtaposes the (giant) Brobdingnagians with the (minuscule) Lilliputians of the first book:

> I reflected what a mortification it must prove to me to appear as inconsiderable in this nation as one single Lilliputian would be among us. But this I conceived was to be the least of my misfortunes: for, as human creatures are observed to be more savage and cruel in proportion to their bulk, what could I expect but to be a morsel in the mouth of the first among these enormous barbarians who should happen to seize me? Undoubtedly philosophers are in the right when they tell us, that nothing is great or small otherwise than by comparison.[11]

DOI: 10.1057/9781137399823.0004

Of course, the speaker is the satirized narrator, who, as a proud and thoroughgoing egoist, effectively misuses comparison, never allowing it to render judgment on himself. His statement regarding comparison, though, speaks truth, although it easily gets lost amidst so much conceit, arrogance, and misunderstanding. *Swift* then proceeds with little other than comparisons, ending the *Travels* with not only that between the Houyhnhnms and the Yahoos but that of both and humankind, as represented in the Portuguese sea captain Don Pedro de Mendez, the first person Gulliver meets upon leaving the land of the "rational animals" and one both reasonable and sensible (even, to invoke Eliot once more, caring and not-caring).

Comparison, it is critical to observe, does not entail, lead to, or result in relativism (as the statement in *Gulliver's Travels* may appear to suggest). Instead, comparison is related to "way," such that, for instance, the way to knowledge of the present is by way of—that is, in, through, and by means of—the past. In comparing in order to know, you do not refer to a transcendent source, where knowledge is thought to lie, above and beyond present considerations. Instead, given the Incarnation, you bring (any) transcendence into time, the abstract into the concrete and particular, where it functions (then) as an immanent source of measurement. In other words, you judge and measure within, by a present standard, here and now ("present" referring to the temporal and to spatial proximity). Knowledge there is, but of a special sort, never unitary but always involving two, in relation, in measurement, and in judgment.

Stephen Dedalus, we will see, separates himself from family, country, church, friends, and "reality," going it alone. Lemuel Gulliver, similarly, separates himself from wife and children repeatedly, and at the end of his self-enforced travels to strange lands, where he constantly compares (though, as I said, very rarely if ever involving himself), he effectively separates himself from "humanity," opting, suspiciously, to spend his time with horses (at the end, consorting even with the "sorrel mare"). Indeed, more than once, Gulliver refuses to observe his own features in the (metaphorical and real) mirror.

Our act of comparing this Romantic novelistic figure with this Enlightenment satirical figure may, then, allow a kind of knowing of each unavailable if we were to consider Stephen and Gulliver each by himself. More important, we will compare Gulliver's and Stephen's self-understanding with that of their authors, a very different matter, indeed.[12]

DOI: 10.1057/9781137399823.0004

Notes

1 T.S. Eliot, *Four Quartets* (New York: Harcourt, Brace, 1943).

2 T.S. Eliot, *The Sacred Wood: Essays on Poetry and Criticism* (London: Methuen, 1920), 33 ("the tools of the critic," says Eliot).

3 See J. Middleton Murry, *Jonathan Swift: A Critical Biography* (London: Jonathan Cape, 1954).

4 T.S. Eliot, *Ash-Wednesday: Six Poems* (New York: Putnam 1930).

5 T.S. Eliot, "Ulysses, Order, and Myth," *Dial* 75 (Nov. 1923), 480–83.

6 Jacques Derrida, "Border Lines: Living On," trans. James Hulbert, in *Deconstruction and Criticism*, by Harold Bloom, Paul de Man, Jacques Derrida, Geoffrey Hartman, and J. Hillis Miller (New York: Seabury P., 1979), 154.

7 Martin Lockerd, review of my *T.S. Eliot and the Essay: From "The Sacred Wood" to "Four Quartets,"* in *Time Present: The Newsletter of the T.S. Eliot Society*, 77 (Summer 2012), 5–6.

8 G.K. Chesterton, "A Piece of Chalk," in *The Art of the Personal Essay*, ed. Phillip Lopate (New York: Anchor-Doubleday, 1994), 250.

9 Eliot, *The Sacred Wood*, 27–28.

10 Ibid., 33, 45.

11 Jonathan Swift, *"Gulliver's Travels" and Other Writings*, ed. Louis A. Landa (Boston, MA: Riverside-Houghton Mifflin, 1960), 70.

12 For helpful, contextualizing studies of *Gulliver's Travels*, see Samuel Holt Monk, "The Pride of Lemuel Gulliver," *Sewanee Review*, 63 (1955), 48–71; James Clifford, "Gulliver's Final Voyage: 'Hard' and 'Soft' Schools of Interpretation," in *Quick Springs of Sense: Studies in the Eighteenth Century*, ed. Larry Champion (Athens: U of Georgia P, 1974), 33–49; Deborah Wyrick, *Jonathan Swift and the Vested Word* (Chapel Hill: U of North Carolina P, 1988); Claude Rawson, *God, Gulliver, and Genocide: Barbarism and the European Imagination, 1492–1945* (Oxford: Oxford UP, 2001); *Gulliver's Travels*: The Norton Critical Edition, ed. Albert J. Rivero, 3rd edn (New York: Norton: 2001); Christopher Fox, ed., *The Cambridge Companion to Jonathan Swift* (Cambridge: Cambridge UP, 2003); and my *Swift's Satires on Modernism: Battlegrounds of Reading and Writing* (New York: Palgrave Macmillan, 2012).

   For similarly helpful studies of *A Portrait of the Artist as a Young Man*, see Wayne C. Booth, *The Rhetoric of Fiction* (Chicago, IL: U of Chicago P, 1961); Weldon Thornton, *The Antimodernism of Joyce's "A Portrait of the Artist as a Young Man"* (Syracuse, NY: Syracuse UP, 1994); Mark Wollaeger, ed., *James Joyce's "A Portrait of the Artist as a Young Man": A Casebook* (Oxford: Oxford UP, 2003); Derek Attridge, ed., *The Cambridge Companion to James Joyce*, 2nd edn. (Cambridge: Cambridge UP, 2004); and John Paul Riquelme, ed., *A Portrait of the Artist as a Young Man*. The Norton Critical Edition (New York: Norton, 2007).

DOI: 10.1057/9781137399823.0004

3

The Flight of Man, the Fall of Icarus and Phaeton

Abstract: *Reading* Gulliver's Travels *and* A Portrait of the Artist as a Young Man, *two of the greatest, most capacious, most perspicacious narratives (and satires) in English, confronts the reader with the problems the protagonists exacerbate, notably including that of separation. Stephen Dedalus, Joyce's semi-autobiographical "hero," reveals a pattern of unchanging response to the world, its stench, and its difficulties: he flees, at the end leaving behind his biological mother, his mother church, and his mother country for a world "forged" in his imagination. In similar fashion, Lemuel Gulliver, a "projector" of sorts and an insatiable explorer and empiricist, even leaves his wife "big with child," returning home at the end, after four voyages, only to separate himself from his family, preferring the company of horses, whom he had come so much to admire in his journey to Houyhnhnmland. Flying, Stephen and Gulliver both* fall, *a fact figured in their stories by respective references to Icarus and Phaeton.*

Atkins, G. Douglas. *Swift, Joyce, and the Flight from Home: Quests of Transcendence and the Sin of Separation.* New York: Palgrave Macmillan, 2014.
DOI: 10.1057/9781137399823.0005.

DOI: 10.1057/9781137399823.0005

> When the soul of a man is born in this country there are nets flung at it to hold it back from flight. You talk to me of nationality, language, religion. I shall try to fly by those nets.
>
> James Joyce, *A Portrait of the Artist as a Young Man*
>
> He was an honest man, and a good sailor, but a little too positive in his own opinions, which was the cause of his destruction, as it hath been of several others. For if he had followed my advice, he might at this time have been safe at home with his family as well as myself.
>
> Jonathan Swift, *Gulliver's Travels*

Joyce's semi-autobiographical novel *A Portrait of the Artist as a Young Man* (1916) ends with the diary entries of the protagonist Stephen Dedalus, from whom his author thus effectually separates himself (as he did in changing the title from *Stephen Hero*). Stephen proudly proclaims, in an ironic embrace of what he calls "life," that he goes forth—to France, we learn from *Ulysses* (1922)—to "encounter for the millionth time the reality of experience and to forge in the smithy of my soul the uncreated conscience of my race."[1] Rarely if ever has a fictional character been so presumptuous or so arrogant.

Unless it be Lemuel Gulliver (le mule), who has stubbornly adhered for many years to his waywardness to the detriment of his family and who, finally back home for the last time in his "little garden at Redriff," lashes out at human pride without the slightest hint of his own complicity and with resolutely no capacity for self-consciousness, making all too clear his desire to separate himself utterly and completely from the humanity that he disparages:

> My reconcilement to the yahoo-kind in general might not be so difficult if they would be content with those vices and follies only which nature hath entitled them to. I am not in the least provoked at the sight of a lawyer, a pickpocket, a colonel, a fool, a lord, a gamester, a politician, a whoremonger, a physician, an evidence, a suborner, an attorney, a traitor, or the like; this is all according to the due course of things: but when I behold a lump of deformity and diseases both in body and mind, smitten with pride, it immediately breaks all the measures of my patience; neither shall I be ever able to comprehend how such an animal and such a vice could tally together. The wise and virtuous Houyhnhnms, who abound in all excellencies that can adorn a rational creature, have no name for this

DOI: 10.1057/9781137399823.0005

vice in their language, which hath no terms to express any thing that is evil, except those whereby they describe the detestible qualities of their yahoos, among which they were not able to distinguish this of pride, for want of thoroughly understanding human nature, as it showeth itself in other countries, where that animal presides. But I, who have had more experience, could plainly observe some rudiments of it among the wild yahoos.[2]

The rational horses have no comparative knowledge. It is ironic that Gulliver, privileged to visit so many different lands and ways of life, thus blessed with comparative opportunities aplenty, fails so miserably at apt measurement and judgment, ever able to exempt himself from criticism. As blind as he is to himself, Gulliver stands fully exposed—and guilty— before Swift's unblinking eyes and ours, his readers'.

Stephen is pictured, time and again, as standing over against others: thus, as the climactic beach scene begins to unfold at the end of the fourth chapter, Joyce tells us of Stephen's separation from his calling, bantering friends: "But he, apart from them and in silence, remembered in what dread he stood of the mystery of his own body."[3] Indeed, these last words point to Stephen's enduring problems with matters of the flesh, more than that, anything material or "physical." A couple of pages later, Stephen is again represented as "alone," a fact Joyce here emphasizes as he places him in the imaginary realms he so dearly craves: "He was alone. He was unheeded, happy and near to the wild heart of life. He was alone and young and wilful and wildhearted, alone amid a waste of wild air and brackish waters....."[4]

Stephen's separation and isolation are nothing new. Even when he was at six in school at Clongowes for the first time, the other boys "seemed to him very strange."[5] Repeatedly, he feels "small and weak,"[6] a condition that makes him forever, in one friend's words, "an antisocial being, wrapped up in yourself."[7] A little older, and "The noise of children at play annoyed him and their silly voices made him feel, even more keenly than he had felt at Clongowes, that he was different from others."[8] Not at all surprisingly, his conversations with friends, particularly in the last chapter, are little other than lectures, and he winds up confessing to Cranly: "I do not fear to be alone or to be spurned for another or to leave whatever I have to leave." Cranly responds: "Alone, quite alone. You have no fear of that. And you know what that word means? Not only to be separate from all others but to have not even one friend," to which Stephen replies, "I will take the risk."[9]

DOI: 10.1057/9781137399823.0005

Sad to say, Stephen is not much of a risk-taker, given to repeating an essential pattern of response. It begins as early as his first days at Clowgowes when he is pushed into a cesspool by one of the other boys; as a result, he gets sick: "sick in his heart."[10] Subsequently, "the world" repulses him, its filth and brutishness repellent and horrible to his ever-sensitive constitution and sensibility. For example, still a lad, when Stephen and Aubrey take a ride in a milkcar, they come upon the quite ordinary sight of cows at grass, and we receive the following insight, including the clear rhyme Joyce makes of Stephen's heart-sickness at school with his acquaintance with the material side of things:

> While the men were milking the boys would take turns in riding the tractable mare round the field. But when autumn came the cows were driven home from the grass: and the first sight of the filthy cowyard at Stradbrook with its foul green puddles and clots of liquid dung and steaming brantroughs sickened Stephen's heart. The cattle which had seemed to him so beautiful in the country on sunny days revolted him and he could not even look at the milk they yielded.[11]

Only slightly less disturbing are Stephen's thoughts—imaginings, really—somewhat later when repulsion at physicality sends him off into paroxysms of transformations of the offensive into the satisfying—he is given, incidentally, to thinking of women as either Marian figures or whores. Typically, the ugly engenders the opposite imagining.

> The names of articles of dress worn by women or of certain soft and delicate stuffs used in their making brought always to his mind a delicate and sinful perfume. As a boy he had imagined the reins by which horses are driven as slender silken bands and it shocked him to feel at Stradbrook the greasy leather of harness. It had shocked him too when he had felt for the first time beneath his tremulous fingers the brittle texture of a woman's stocking for, retaining nothing of all he read save that which seemed to him an echo or prophecy of his own state, it was only amid softworded phrases or within rosesoft stuffs that he dared to conceive of the soul or body of a woman moving with tender life.[12]

What Lemuel Gulliver flees from is less certain. At first, he says he set sail, as a ship's surgeon, for financial reasons, his business on land having failed to prosper (and Gulliver shows intense signs of interest in money, deciding to marry in order "to alter my condition" for the better).[13] But in Part II, he says he was "condemned by nature and fortune to an active and restless life."[14] About his third voyage, Gulliver goes into more detail,

DOI: 10.1057/9781137399823.0005

describing the commander of the *Hope-well*'s several importunings and promises, concluding that he "could not reject his proposal; the thirst I had of seeing the world, notwithstanding my past misfortunes, continuing as violent as ever."[15] Finally, in beginning his account of his last voyage, Gulliver says, feeling no shame and little regret, that he "left my poor wife big with child, and accepted an advantageous offer made to be captain of the *Adventurer*."[16]

As the introductory accounts for all the voyages attest, Gulliver is a man of few feelings and a great interest in material things (not, of course, those material things that send Stephen Dedalus flying off in search of transcendent realms). Gulliver observes, he quantifies, and he faithfully describes the superficies of things. So much the observer and would-be scientist is he that, in Brobdingnag, unfazed by the past danger, he scruples immediately to measure precisely the tail of the enormous rat that he had out of self-defense to dispatch with his "hanger."[17]

With his empiricist eye ever trained on observable details, Gulliver proudly acknowledges, in the third part, his deep interest in and engagement with "projects," theoretical and supposedly scientific experiments widely belittled for their abstraction and uselessness. Indeed, the sole Ancient in a world populated and run by Moderns, Lord Munodi "was pleased to represent me as a great admirer of projects, and a person of much curiosity and easy belief, which indeed was not without truth, for I had been a sort of projector in my younger days."[18] Gulliver is, as his name suggests, gullible, and despite—or perhaps because of—his empiricism manifested in curiosity and a love of measurements, he is readily taken in. His commitments appear in his prose style, notably in the third chapter of "A Voyage to Laputa, Etc.," where, in highly technical form, he describes the operations of "the floating island," used—pre-*1984*—for the suppression of dissent and opposition to the king's rule.[19] Not surprisingly, then, Gulliver is smitten with the "projects" underway in the Grand Academy of Lagado, including the extraction of sunbeams from cucumbers, the reduction of human excrement to its "original food," and a new method of construction consisting of "beginning at the roof and working downwards to the foundation."[20] He is similarly taken with the experiments in "speculative learning," notably including those working on *res et verba*; in fact, in the school of languages, Gulliver discovers a project "to shorten discourse by cutting polysyllables into one, and leaving out verbs and participles, because in reality all things imaginable are but nouns."[21] This project connects

DOI: 10.1057/9781137399823.0005

with then-current efforts in Swift's own time, efforts with catastrophic consequences. The dim-witted nominalist and materialist Gulliver describes the effort in some detail: this project, he says, which also looks toward the last book of the *Travels*—typically, he is unaware of implications and problems—

> was a scheme for entirely abolishing all words whatsoever; and this was urged as a great advantage in point of health as well as brevity. For it is plain that every word we speak is in some degree a diminution of our lungs by corrosion, and consequently contributes to the shortening of our lives. An expedient was therefore offered, that since words are only names for *things*, it would be more convenient for all men to carry about them such *things* as were necessary to express the particular business they are to discourse on.[22]

This unlikely and unseemly project is the work of learned *men*, like those earlier described as having their heads so far in the air that they require servants equipped with "flappers" to knock some sense into them and bring them back down to earth (Swift will, in a bit, literalize the metaphor, a favorite gambit of his, with "the floating island" Laputa, whose Spanish meaning he obviously invokes).

The men here differ radically from the women, whose values and interests are healthily material, physical, and natural. Blessed with "abundance of vivacity," the women embrace strangers and openly carry on with them, their husbands completely oblivious while absorbed in their "projects." "The wives and daughters," says Gulliver, who shows little interest in his own, and no awareness of the absurd impossibility of his words, "lament their confinement to the island, although I think it the most delicious spot of ground in the world."[23] It is precisely the women who represent objection, and an (Ancient) alternative to modern abstraction: the expedient of substituting things for words (and making matters "easy," always a prime value for Swift's antagonists), this "invention,"

> would certainly have taken place, to the great ease as well as health of the subject, if the women in conjunction with the vulgar and illiterate had not threatened to raise a rebellion, unless they might be allowed the liberty to speak with their tongues, after the manner of their forefathers; such constant irreconcilable enemies to science are the common people.[24]

These people, women and common folk, stand opposed, then, to "the most learned and wise," as well as to Lemuel Gulliver, ship's surgeon, husband, and father: "*splendide mendax*."[25] The issues could hardly be clearer, given in these stark terms.

DOI: 10.1057/9781137399823.0005

As I have already suggested in passing, Gulliver is an Enlightenment figure, representing the values and primacy of (disembodied) reason. He is thus forward-looking, a pale but nevertheless clearly identifiable avatar of the senseless speaker of "A Modest Proposal": insouciant, detached, clinical, reasonable, and a-moral.[26] On the side of science and pitted against its "enemies," women and common folk, he has no faith that the unenlightened can possibly be intersected by judicious and wise understanding. For him, they amount, therefore, to little more than throw-aways, essentially what he practices after converting to horsiness following his last voyage and neglecting, denying, and literally separating himself from wife and children. Lemuel Gulliver *is* either/or.

He does not, to be sure, lack a comparative sense, frequently, in fact, comparing conditions, practices, mores, and laws in his adopted country to those back home in England, usually to the detriment of the latter. For Gulliver, the known and the familiar offer no valid standard of measurement, gullible as he is, a thoroughly modern Modern. The voyage to Houyhnhnmland provides a final chance to compare and to learn. Gulliver screws it up. Nowhere is this clearer or more significant than when, effectively expelled by the horses he adores, he is rescued by a human being who, like him, in many ways resembles the detested Yahoos and (yet) acts like a rational being: not a "rational animal," but as Swift put it in a letter to his friend Pope as he was completing *Gulliver's Travels*, an animal *"rationis capax."*[27] Don Pedro de Mendez, Portuguese sea-captain, shows himself to be not just capable of reason but a human animal compassionate and generous. Gulliver, though, fails to see that Don Pedro is something of a *via media* between the beloved horses and the disgusting Yahoos, and effectively dismisses him, from his supposedly superior point of view and acquisition of the tools of enlightenment, as one with "very good *human* understanding."[28]

Gulliver has, of course, heard other helpful voices in the lands he has visited, including that of Lord Munodi and that of the king of Brobdingnag, but even as he engages in ready comparison of his new situation with conditions back home, he fails to apply the measurement to himself. His failure is literalized at the end of the visit to Brobdingnag (and repeated back home finally, at the end of Book Four). Gulliver's incapacity appears, indeed, in striking relief at the end of the second book, after he is rescued, the captain of the ship that picks him up, a Shropshire man, wondering why he speaks

DOI: 10.1057/9781137399823.0005

so loud, asking me whether the King or Queen of that country were thick of hearing. I told him it was what I had been used to for above two years past, and that I admired as much at the voices of him and his men, who seemed to me only to whisper, and yet I could hear them well enough. . . . I told him. . . that when I first got into the ship, and the sailors stood all about me, I thought they were the most little contemptible creatures I had ever beheld [an echo of the King of Brobdingnag's famous denunciation of humankind, himself, as Gulliver notes, a victim of inexperience, with no bases for comparison]. For, indeed, while I was in that prince's country, I could never endure to look in a glass after my eyes had been accustomed to such prodigious objects, because the comparison gave me so despicable a conceit of my self.[29]

Gulliver adds that, in Brobdingnag, in face of the enormous creatures, "I winked at my own littleness"—essentially a petty Lilliputian—"as people do at their own faults." Then Gulliver adduces the captain's mirth at his "fall from so great an height into the sea," which *he* describes via "the comparison of Phaeton," a judgment of which Gulliver had never thought, though it was "so obvious" to his rescuer "that he could not forbear applying it, although I did not much admire the conceit."[30] Even when judged, Gulliver remains largely unaffected, deflecting and minimizing the critique. Unable to look at himself, Gulliver closes off self-criticism.

Pattern thus seems clear in Gulliver's way of thinking and responding. In rather more sophisticated fashion (as one might expect from what is obviously a novel and a highly sophisticated one, at that), *A Portrait of the Artist as a Young Man* does much more with pattern, foregrounding it, in fact. The novel is constructed on and as a pattern of response, representing movement becoming pattern and thus acquiring meaning. That construction or structure is exactly what Eliot describes in "Burnt Norton," first of *Four Quartets*: "Only by the form, the pattern,/ Can words or music reach/ The stillness." He adds: "The detail of the pattern is movement."[31]

What Joyce highlights in *A Portrait* is Stephen's essential, repeated, never-transcended pattern of response to slight, injustice, the foul-smelling, in short, the physical aspect of human nature and human life (never mind such bestiality as the extreme Yahoos represent in *Gulliver's Travels*). He gets sick (in his heart), sometimes rebels, in the end flees, trying his best to get away and separate himself from all that he detests and reviles.

DOI: 10.1057/9781137399823.0005

That pattern, which Joyce exploits novelistically, is easily recognizable as Incarnational, although I do not suggest that he invoked it as such, or even recognized it in those terms. That he most likely did not does not in the least throw its existence and function into question. Incarnational pattern is timeless and universal, "always already" there and available for apprehension, although God saw that the paradigmatic instance of It, *the* Incarnation, was necessary in order for readily misunderstanding humankind to get it right. And even then, we but half-understand.

Notes

1   James Joyce, *A Portrait of the Artist as a Young Man*, 1916 (New York: Viking-Penguin, 1964), 253.
2   Jonathan Swift, *"Gulliver's Travels" and Other Writings*, ed. Louis A. Landa (Boston, MA: Riverside-Houghton Mifflin, 1960), 238–39.
3   Ibid., 168.
4   Ibid., 171.
5   Ibid., 13.
6   Ibid., 8, 17.
7   Ibid., 177.
8   Ibid., 65.
9   Ibid., 247.
10   Ibid., 13.
11   Ibid., 64–65.
12   Ibid., 155.
13   Ibid., 15.
14   Ibid., 67.
15   Ibid., 123.
16   Ibid., 179.
17   Ibid., 75–76.
18   Ibid., 145.
19   Ibid., 135.
20   Ibid., 146.
21   Ibid., 150.
22   Ibid.
23   Ibid., 133.
24   Ibid., 150–51.
25   Ibid., 151. The phrase appears on the title page of the 1735 edition of *Travels*.
26   See my discussion of "A Modest Proposal" in *Reading Essays: An Invitation* (Athens: U of Georgia P, 2008), 55–61.

DOI: 10.1057/9781137399823.0005

27 Swift, 494 (letter of September 29, 1725).
28 Ibid., 233.
29 Ibid., 119.
30 Ibid., 120.
31 T.S. Eliot, *Four Quartets* (New York: Harcourt, Brace, 1943).

DOI: 10.1057/9781137399823.0005

4

The Flying or Floating Island: Lemuel Gulliver and Ideas Disembodied

Abstract: *Lemuel Gulliver's desires are figured in his immediate and unstinting embrace of life on Laputa, the Floating or Flying Island, in Book Three of the* Travels. *Written last of the four, the third book of* Gulliver's Travels *brilliantly satirizes modern thought and experimental science, its assumptions and its implications. As Swift sees it, modernity seeks little less than transcendence of the human. This, and more, he represents in his narrator's thoughtless embrace of Laputa (meaning "whore"). The inhabitants of Laputa and of the subjugated world beneath them are given to abstraction and the theoretical, and as a consequence nothing actually* works—*except on the separated estate below of Lord Munodi, an exemplary Ancient in this relentless battle of the books. For the Laputans, as for other peoples visited in Book Three, there is strangeness without reality, reason separated from common sense.*

Atkins, G. Douglas. *Swift, Joyce, and the Flight from Home: Quests of Transcendence and the Sin of Separation.* New York: Palgrave Macmillan, 2014. DOI: 10.1057/9781137399823.0006.

DOI: 10.1057/9781137399823.0006

If you have built castles in the air, your work need not be lost, that is where they should be Now put the foundations under them.

Henry David Thoreau, *Walden*

What is permanent and good in Romanticism is curiosity—a curiosity which recognizes that any life, if accurately and profoundly penetrated, is interesting and always strange. Romanticism is a short cut to the strangeness without the reality, and it leads its disciples only back upon themselves.

T.S. Eliot, *The Sacred Wood*

In Book Three of his *Travels*, Lemuel Gulliver visits Laputa, the Flying or Floating Island—at least, first he does, for unlike all the other parts, this book contains several outlying voyages. He is privileged to see the Grand Academy of Lagado, where, amid other perverse "projects," he encounters "a most ingenious architect who had contrived a new method for building houses, by beginning at the roof and working downwards to the foundation, which he justified to me by the like practice of those two prudent insects, the bee and the spider."[1] With this last reference, Swift's reader thinks immediately of the early satire *The Battle of the Books*, in which those two insects represent Ancients and Moderns, respectively.[2] The world of Laputa is awash in modernism, itself an outgrowth of Romanticism with—according to T.S. Eliot—its commitment to strangeness without the reality.[3]

The Laputans are indeed strange: Gulliver says, immediately, that he had "never till then seen a race of mortals so singular in their shapes, habits and countenances. Their heads were all reclined either to the right or the left; one of their eyes turned inward, and the other directly up to the zenith."[4] The servants, many of them, were equipped with "a blown bladder fastened like a flail to the end of a short stick" and filled with "dried pease or little pebbles."[5] With these "flappers" they struck the mouths and ears of those about them, for "the minds of these people are so taken up with intense speculations, that they neither can speak, nor attend to the discourses of others, without being roused by some external taction upon the organs of speech and hearing."[6]

About the Laputans' houses, we are told by Gulliver of their many and serious problems, a passage that opens out to reveal many of the

DOI: 10.1057/9781137399823.0006

principal objects of Swift's scathing and unrelieved satire. This is, indeed, strangeness without reality, wrought with the (parallel) separation of sense and reason, the heads of the Laputans lost (as we just observed) in the air yet in charge and dominating:

> Their houses are very ill built, the walls bevil, without one right angle in any apartment, and this defect ariseth from the contempt they bear for practical geometry, which they despise as vulgar and mechanic, those instructions they give being too refined for the intellectuals of their workmen, which occasions perpetual mistakes. And although they are dextrous enough upon a piece of paper in the management of the rule, the pencil, and the divider, yet in the common actions and behaviour of life I have not seen a more clumsy, awkward, and unhandy people, nor so slow and perplexed in their conceptions upon all other subjects, except those of mathematics and music. They are very bad reasoners, and vehemently given to opposition, unless when they happen to be of the right opinion, which is seldom their case. Imagination, fancy, and invention, they are wholly strangers to, nor have any words in their language by which those ideas can be expressed; the whole compass of their thoughts and mind being shut up within the two forementioned sciences.[7]

Whether or not it is Gulliver's misperception, the Laputans most assuredly are not strangers to "imagination, fancy, and invention"; on the contrary, they are wholly given to them, like the self-engendering spider of *The Battle of the Books*, arch-Modern that it is. That the Laputans, intense specialists in abstraction, the airy, and the disembodied, are also "vehemently given to opposition" is a telling point.

The visiting Gulliver, who had left home this time after not even ten days, lured by the prospects of some wealth and indulging "the thirst I had of seeing the world," which lust he describes as "violent," soon winds up in the hands of pirates.[8] A man of some authority among them was a Dutchman, depicted by Gulliver as the very opposite of Christian, indeed a heathen; he prevails upon the others "to have a punishment inflicted on me, worse in all human appearance than death itself."[9] It entails abject separation, an ironic twist upon Gulliver's fundamental desire.

> My men were sent by an equal division into both the pirate ships, and my sloop new manned. As to my self, it was determined that I should be set adrift in a small canoe, with paddles and a sail, and four days' provisions, which last the Japanese captain was so kind to double out of his own stores, and would permit no man to search me. I got down into the canoe, while

DOI: 10.1057/9781137399823.0006

the Dutchman, standing upon the deck, loaded me with all the curses and injurious terms his language could afford.[10]

Separation here teams up with opposition, both equally violent. Laputa is the flying or floating island hovering over a chosen part of the continent Balnibarbi, whose "metropolis" is the aforementioned Lagado. The island is positioned above an area at the king's discretion, for it effectively serves as an instrument of domination and control. The island is, then, the *head* of which Balnibarbi is the body, subject to the ministrations of that head. Of Laputa, which he had once described as "the most delicious spot of ground in the world" (despite its precisely not being "ground" at all), he grows weary.[11] The ever-curious one being equally credulous, the island at first appealed and attracted, and it *could have been* that Gulliver would see himself in these people. But *they* are not curious, and Gulliver soon decides to separate himself from them too, including literally, his sense of self-importance once again asserting itself (even as he unwittingly joins with the women in feeling neglected):

> Although I cannot say that I was ill treated in this island, yet I must confess I thought my self too much neglected, not without some degree of contempt. For neither prince nor people appeared to be curious in any part of knowledge, except mathematics and music, wherein I was far their inferior, and upon that account very little regarded.[12]

For Gulliver, "projector" and would-be scientist and arch-empiricist, curiosity is perhaps the prime value—unless it be "my self."

In Lagado, Gulliver comes upon the Grand Academy, with its (absurd) experiments and "speculative learning," and seems to fit right in. He thus stands in opposition to Lord Munodi, whose Ancient ways conflict to his detriment with those of (modern) science. Surely a "mouth-piece" of Swift, a thesis to the satirical antithesis, this noble (and estimable) figure lives "retired" from the world, which certainly views him with far more contempt than they display toward the prickly and needy Gulliver. Gulliver has to admit that "every thing about [his host] was magnificent, regular, and polite."[13] Lord Munodi's account of Laputa offers a thoroughgoing critique of all that Gulliver has just observed—but did not *measure*, his attention being wholly empirical rather than moral or even intellectual. Munodi's discourse is historical in garb, but rife with ethical and political critique, a powerful combination, unavailable to Gulliver. It is a continuation of Swift's attack on (modern) enthusiasm pervasive in *A Tale of a Tub*, where it accounts for all "revolutions" in government, philosophy, and religion.[14] It is nothing short of a utopian vision (in Eric Voegelin's trenchant terms, "the immanentization of the eschaton"):[15]

> The sum of his discourse was to this effect. That about forty years ago, certain persons went up to Laputa either upon business or diversion, and after five months continuance came back with a very little smattering in mathematics, but full of volatile spirits acquired in that airy region. That these persons upon their return began to dislike the management of everything below, and fell into schemes of putting all arts, sciences, languages, and mechanics upon a new foot. To this end they procured a royal patent for erecting an academy of PROJECTORS in Lagado; and the humour prevailed so strongly among the people, that there is not a town of any consequence in the kingdom without such an academy. In these colleges the professors contrive new rules and methods of agriculture and building, and new instruments and tools for all trades and manufactures, whereby, as they undertake, one man shall do the work of ten; a place may be built in a week, of materials so durable as to last for ever without repairing.[16]

Rather than a (Christian) intersection of timelessness with time, here human invention represents, in rather literal fashion, transcendence wrenched into immanence, transforming the temporal, and thus leaving but one-half standing, that created world that has usurped the place of the natural and the given, remaking it in man's own sordid, selfish image. The picture is all too familiar to us who have managed to survive the twentieth century (and who might see in Swift's prescient words both an analysis of our present world and an alternative to its pervasive falsehoods, abject horrors, and widespread and intense sufferings):

> All the fruits of the earth shall come to maturity at whatever season we think fit to choose, and increase an hundred fold more than they do at present, with innumerable other happy proposals. The only inconvenience is, that none of these projects are yet brought to perfection, and in the mean time the whole country lies miserably waste, the houses in ruins, and the people without food or clothes. By all which, instead of being discouraged, they are fifty times more violently bent upon prosecuting their schemes, driven equally on by hope and despair; that as for himself [Lord Munodi], being not of an enterprising spirit, he was content to go on in the old forms, to live in the houses his ancestors had built, and act as they did in every part of life without innovation. That some few other persons of quality and gentry had done the same, but were looked on with an eye of contempt and ill will, as enemies to art, ignorant, and ill commonwealth's men, preferring their own ease and sloth before the general improvement of their country.[17]

DOI: 10.1057/9781137399823.0006

Amidst the abstractions, this "discourse" is concrete and pointedly useful.

"Sovegna vos," writes Eliot in *Ash-Wednesday*.[18] Lord Munodi's separation from (modern) madness is a positive, very different from Gulliver's willful separation from precisely this enforced separation. Swift's skillful, subtle allusion to "commonwealth's men" points to both political manipulation of ideas and language and the (true) way by which matters are made indeed complex and complicated, truth intersecting with falsehood.

In due course, Gulliver's consuming curiosity leads him well beyond Balnibarbi and the academies of Lagado, as "delicious" as they are. Abruptly, and in a one-sentence paragraph unusual in the *Travels*, Gulliver declares, after faithfully describing his observations of the Grand Academy, "I saw nothing in this country that could invite me to a longer continuance, and began to think of returning home to England."[19] Possibly quite enough said to reveal a great deal.

What follows, here in Part Three, which was written last, enhances the representations earlier. This book is often judged to be of lesser quality than the other three, different from them, it is alleged, in being in certain ways diffuse, the travels, after all, not being confined to one spot, but many. I, however, think "A Voyage to Laputa, Etc." both important and artful. Its place in the *Travels* reminds me of the place of "The Dry Salvages" in *Four Quartets*, where it occupies the same position and clearly serves to make clear Eliot's central thematic and rhetorical charge, that regarding Incarnation as "The hint half guessed, the gift half understood."[20] Part Three of *Gulliver's Travels*, in similar structural fashion, brings modern (mis)understandings to the fore, making explicit what is certainly at least implicit elsewhere in the great satire.

In the event, Gulliver travels to Maldonada, thence immediately to Glubbdubdrib, that is, the "Island of *Sorcerers* or *Magicians*,"[21] which situation hardly seems accidental on Swift's part. The opportunity given is turned by Gulliver into a bastardized trip to "the kingdom of the dead," an ironic take-off on Odysseus's climactic visit where his education begins in the purgation of his egoism and willfulness; Odysseus, in short, *learns* from his conversations with the dead. Allowed to call up any persons he wishes from among the dead, Gulliver reveals his extreme pettiness: he completely botches the major opportunity he is given, reducing it in ways not tragic but both bathetic and pathetic while accentuating

DOI: 10.1057/9781137399823.0006

his insouciance and blind egoism—note again the kind of details that Gulliver notices and so provides us in his account:

> I made my humble acknowledgements to his Highness [the Governor] for so great a favour. We were in a chamber, from whence there was a fair prospect into the park. And because my first inclination was to be entertained with scenes of pomp and magnificence, I desired to see Alexander the Great, at the head of his army just after the battle of Arbela, which upon a motion of the Governor's finger immediately appeared in a large field under the window, where we stood. Alexander was called up into the room: it was with great difficulty that I understood his Greek, and had but little of my own. He assured me upon his honour that he was not poisoned, but died of a fever by excessive drinking.
>
> Next I saw Hannibal passing the Alps, who told me he had not a drop of vinegar in his camp.[22]

Following even briefer representations of seeing Caesar, Pompey, and Brutus, Gulliver concludes the chapter with these words:

> It would be tedious to trouble the reader with relating what vast numbers of illustrious persons were called up, to gratify that insatiable desire I had to see the world in every period of antiquity placed before me. I chiefly fed my eyes with beholding the destroyers of tyrants and usurpers, and the restorers of liberty to oppressed and injured nations. But it is impossible to express the satisfaction I received in my own mind, after such a manner as to make it a suitable entertainment to the reader.[23]

The goal of entertainment for the reader matches Gulliver's goal of satisfaction, itself, according to *A Tale of a Tub*, a prime modern desire.

In a separate chapter, the journey to Glubbdubdrib continues, the focus now on ancient and modern history and the misleading interpretations perpetrated by "prostitute writers," and the whoring after position and power that characterizes that sordid history. His curiosity somewhat abated, Gulliver expresses dismay and disgust and professes disillusionment concerning "persons of high rank."[24]

Gulliver then heads for Luggnagg, which he understands as a pathway to Japan and, ultimately, a way back home to England; he stays three months. He describes the Luggnaggians as "a polite and courteous people," with "some share of that pride which is peculiar to all eastern countries," a striking instance of no doubt growing cultural xenophobia. Here, Gulliver finds himself in the land of the *struldbruggs* or *immortals*. Even before he meets *them*, the ever-credulous, ever-enthusiastic Gulliver

DOI: 10.1057/9781137399823.0006

cried out as in a rapture: Happy nation where every child hath at least a chance for being immortal! Happy people who enjoy so many living examples of ancient virtue, and have masters ready to instruct them in the wisdom of all former ages. But happiest beyond all comparison are those excellent *struldbruggs*, who being born exempt from that universal calamity of human nature, have their minds free and disengaged, without the weight and depression of spirits caused by the continual apprehension of death.[25]

This is another variant of the visit to "the kingdom of the dead," a modern re-interpretation, as it were, cleansed of apparent difficulties and rendered free of such ethical and intellectual necessities as personal growth, change, and development: all is yours for the taking. It is clear, moreover, that Part Three of *Gulliver's Travels* is, indeed, an encyclopedic analysis of modern thought and desire, themselves revealed as a quest of the transformation—or transcendence—of little less than human nature. In fact, modernism emerges as the attempt to bypass or, better, to deny death.

Gulliver's quickly stated desire is "to pass my life here in the conversation of those superior beings the *struldbruggs*, if they would please to admit me."[26] The question is put to him, "how I should employ my self and pass the time if I were sure to live for ever."[27] Gulliver says, shamelessly, "it was easy to be eloquent on so copious and delightful a subject, especially to me who have been often apt to amuse my self with visions of what I should do if I were a king, a general, or a great lord."[28] He then launches into a lengthy and detailed declaration of what he would do if born an "immortal," another instance of such speculation into which he always gladly enters. The shameless egoism is virtually unmatchable.

if it had been my fortune to come into the world a *struldbrugg*, as soon as I could discover my own happiness by understanding the difference between life and death, I would first resolve by all arts and methods whatsoever to procure my self riches. In the pursuit of which by thrift and management, I might reasonably expect in about two hundred years to be the wealthiest man in the kingdom. In the second place, I would from my earliest youth apply myself to the study of arts and sciences, by which I should arrive in time to excel all others in learning. Lastly, I would carefully record every action and event of consequence that happened in the public, impartially draw the characters of the several successions of princes, and great ministers of state, with my own observations on every point. I would exactly set down the several changes in customs, languages, fashions of dress, diet and diversions. By all which acquirements, I should

DOI: 10.1057/9781137399823.0006

be a living treasury of knowledge and wisdom, and certainly become the oracle of the nation.[29]

Other schemes immediately follow, led by this one: "I would never marry after threescore, but live in an hospitable manner, yet still on the saving side."[30]

This account by Gulliver generates "some laughter at my expense,"[31] which stems from the nature and condition of this "immortality." It is not at all what Gulliver had immediately supposed, and so he has to be set straight:

> ...the system of living contrived by me was unreasonable and unjust, because it supposed a perpetuity of youth, health, and vigour, which no man could be so foolish to hope, however extravagant he might be in his wishes.... [T]he question therefore was not whether a man would choose to be always in the prime of youth, attended with prosperity and health, but how he would pass a perpetual life under all the usual disadvantages which old age brings along with it.[32]

Gulliver's interpreter adds, as if the come-uppance is not yet sufficient,

> ... [A]lthough few men will avow their desires of being immortal upon such hard conditions, yet in the two kingdoms...of Balnibarbi and Japan, he observed that every man desired to put off death for some time longer, let it approach ever so late, and he rarely heard of any man who died willingly, except he were incited by the extremity of grief or torture. And he appealed to me whether in those countries I had traveled, as well as my own, I had not observed the same general disposition.[33]

Next comes a depressing catalogue of all those ills and problems that inevitably befall these "immortals" as they age; as a result, "they were not only opinionative, peevish, covetous, morose, vain, talkative, but uncapable of friendship, and dead to all natural affection, which never descended below their grandchildren. Envy and impotent desires are their prevailing passions."[34]

After reciting still more observations of the ills that attend the *struldbruggs*, Gulliver concludes, his initial adjective more telling than he realizes: "They were the most mortifying sight I ever beheld, and the women more horrible than the men. Besides the usual deformities in extreme old age, they acquired an additional ghastliness in proportion to their number of years, which is not to be described."[35] Gulliver then admits that his "keen appetite for perpetuity of life was much abated." He even adds, surprisingly, that he "grew heartily ashamed of the pleasing visions

DOI: 10.1057/9781137399823.0006

I had formed."[36] Still, Gulliver thinks little of trying to *learn from experience*. Thus he says he offers this account of the "immortals" because he thought it "might be some *entertainment* to the reader" (italics added).[37]

After five years and six months away, Gulliver returns to Redriff, detailing the date and time of his arrival and describing what he found there in these minimalist terms: I "found my wife and family in good health."[38]

End of story.

Adaptable man, Lemuel Gulliver admits to wanderlust, without quite knowing what it means. Indeed, he does not know himself, the puling little self that he tries so hard to protect and defend. His *Travels* is a story of egoism and pride, the great subjects of satire.

Gulliver is right about little, so wrong about much. Curious and credulous, he is committed to observing, thus to traveling, notably away from home, which has few attractions for him. He holds facts sacrosanct, measurable and thus true, and so mistakenly assumes that to learn about "the world," he has to venture far and wide, in search of the extraordinary, which he certainly comes upon time and again, over and over. There is no sense at all that, despite his occasional assertion, he could stay home and learn as much if not more. There is no sense, either, that time and place are *attended*—by other times and places.

We may well need experience—comparison tells us so—and the need is borne out by the extremism to which the King of Brobdingnag goes in his denunciations, some of them just, to be sure, but some of them deriving from the kind of parochialism and lack of comparative awareness that also marks the petty Phaiaicians in *The Odyssey* isolated, separate from the world. There *is*, says Eliot in "East Coker," "only a limited value/ In the knowledge derived from experience." It may be, although Gulliver has no clue about it, that knowledge of greater value may come from the experience of books, or at least from examination of the world based on knowledge of something other and more than the measurement of things—best, possibly, from the measurement that comparison with knowledge of, and the past responses of, the dead offers. Gulliver shows, though, that when he is privileged to meet the dead, he asks questions that elicit only the kind of factual answers in which he has all along shown interest.

Blind to Incarnational understanding of time and place, Gulliver accepts our all-too-familiar, endemic acceptance of the separation of

DOI: 10.1057/9781137399823.0006

body and spirit (or soul). Incarnation shows us that and how the Logos becomes flesh, ideas becoming embodied in persons and our acts. It is a revolutionary development, unique in the history of humankind.

The horses, to which Gulliver pledges allegiance and that exist for him as an ideal, are "rational animals." Gulliver's ideal is not, obviously, disembodied here, but instead present in the extra-human (and not all that attractive to the unprejudiced eye). Reason alone Swift shows to be at once unattractive and impossible for us human beings. Don Pedro de Mendez, on the other hand, shows himself *"rationis capax"* and at the same time compassionate and sensible. Gulliver, though, dismisses him precisely because he is human.

According to Swift, humanity has limitations. Science, though, was in the process of "flying by" those limitations, creating worlds of ease and convenience and entertainment, eliminating poverty and inequality and difficulty—all constructed on the dictates of reason, separate from common sense and the wisdom of the ages, floating above and looking down upon doubters, rebels, and reactionaries.

Notes

1   Jonathan Swift, *"Gulliver's Travels" and Other Writings*, ed. Louis A. Landa (Boston, MA: Riverside-Houghton Mifflin, 1960), 146.
2   See my discussion in *Swift's Satires on Modernism: Battlegrounds of Reading and Writing* (New York: Palgrave Macmillan, 2013).
3   T.S. Eliot, *The Sacred Wood: Essays on Poetry and Criticism* (London: Methuen, 1920), 28.
4   Swift, 127.
5   Ibid., 127–28.
6   Ibid., 128.
7   Ibid., 131.
8   Ibid., 123.
9   Ibid., 125.
10 Ibid.
11 Ibid., 133.
12 Ibid., 140.
13 Ibid., 141.
14 See ibid., esp. 327–31.
15 Eric Voegelin, *The New Science of Politics* (Chicago, IL: U of Chicago P, 1952).
16 Swift, 143–44.

DOI: 10.1057/9781137399823.0006

17   Ibid., 144.
18   T.S. Eliot, *Ash-Wednesday: Six Poems* (New York: Putnam, 1930).
19   Swift, 156.
20   T. S. Eliot, *Four Quartets* (New York: Harcourt, Brace, 1943).
21   Swift, 157.
22   Ibid., 158.
23   Ibid., 159.
24   Ibid., 162.
25   Ibid., 167.
26   Ibid., 167–68.
27   Ibid., 168.
28   Ibid.
29   Ibid., 168–69.
30   Ibid., 169.
31   Ibid., 170.
32   Ibid.
33   Ibid., 170–71.
34   Ibid., 171.
35   Ibid., 172–73.
36   Ibid., 173.
37   Ibid.
38   Ibid., 176.

DOI: 10.1057/9781137399823.0006

5

Aesthetics as Asceticism: Stephen Dedalus's Quest of Transcendence

Abstract: *From the beginning of the novel, Stephen Dedalus seeks transcendence of what he later considers "the sluggish matter of the earth." His—anti-Christian— "epiphany" on the beach in Chapter Four confirms his desire of separation, and he ends up there literally loving himself. Stephen, in fact, desires transfiguration, as well as transcendence; he can deal with a "girl" only by changing her, for instance, into the likeness of a delicate and pure seabird. What he seeks, Stephen finds in his imagination, and so the poetry he writes exchanges "ardent ways" for the nebulous creations of that imagination. In similar fashion, he develops and puts forth an aesthetic of transcendence in which emotion is arrested. That impersonal theory thus stems from his own very personal needs, the pattern of which is always present and visible.*

Atkins, G. Douglas. *Swift, Joyce, and the Flight from Home: Quests of Transcendence and the Sin of Separation.* New York: Palgrave Macmillan, 2014.
DOI: 10.1057/9781137399823.0007.

DOI: 10.1057/9781137399823.0007

> —Let us take woman, said Stephen.
> —Let us take her! said Lynch fervently.
>
> The artist, like the God of the creation, remains within or behind or beyond or above his handiwork, invisible, refined out of existence, indifferent, paring his fingernails.
> —Trying to refine them also out of existence, said Lynch.
>
> James Joyce, *A Portrait of the Artist as a Young Man*

Stephen Dedalus has no embodied ideal, such as Lemuel Gulliver finds in the Houyhnhnms. Nor does he discover a Flying or Floating Island, above the earth but, according to Gulliver, "the most delicious spot of ground in the world."[1] Yet Stephen seeks just such a state, forever "weary of ardent ways" (according to the villanelle he composes) and trying hard to transcend "the sluggish matter of the earth."[2] In an epiphantic moment—very nearly the opposite of Incarnationally "attended" moments—Stephen feels "above him the vast indifferent dome and the calm processes of the heavenly bodies; and the earth beneath him, the earth that had borne him, had taken him to her breast."[3] Stephen is an arch-enthusiast, fancy having gotten "astride on his reason," imagination being "at cuffs with the senses, and common understanding, as well as common sense, kicked out of doors."[4] Stephen Dedalus finds—that is, posits—transcendence, purification, and refinement in his imagination, thence in the "art" he will use it to make, "*forg*[ing] in the smithy of my soul the uncreated conscience of my race."[5] Joyce's novel reveals Stephen as Gulliver's chief rival for supremacy in the sordid pantheon of the proud and the egoistic, an Icarian and ultimately Satanic figure of pettiness and meanness, though a diminutive character of gigantic and perverse spiritual proportions.

As I used to confess to students, I hate Stephen Dedalus, and a primary reason is that he so often and profoundly reflects who I am. I am trying, but, despite Old Possum, Swift, and Joyce himself, I still fall victim to the lures of (mere) transcendence; I too am a loner; I too am an egoist. Of course, my personal response affects my interpretation and presentation of Joyce's semi-autobiographical protagonist, so much so that I flout my principal Incarnational arguments: if *I* were true to those principles. I would at least try to see Stephen both critically *and* sympathetically. Intellectually, I acknowledge that his author probably wanted his readers

DOI: 10.1057/9781137399823.0007

to respond in that both/and fashion. I have trouble doing so, however. As Eliot reveals, it is hard for us "Moderns" to "associate" thinking and feeling. I take some comfort here, though, in realizing that my divided and separated response and sensibility confirm the major point that we are likely to "get it" only *half*-right: either admiring Stephen uncritically or condemning him outright, unsympathetically. The temptation appears ingrained.

Stephen's art, such as it is, perfectly reflects its author, his "personality" everywhere present in it despite his vaunted aesthetic claims. We hear first of his poetic writing in the second chapter, following his non-experience with the girl on the tram: she evidently wanted him to kiss her, but he, in the pattern of responding that defines him, does nothing, save for later writing a poem about it all and then going into his mother's bedroom to gaze at himself "for a long time in the mirror of her dressing-table."[6] Stephen's Romanticism appears variously: in his choice of the rebellious Lord Byron as his favorite poet (trying to write his verses, he "knew it was right to begin so"—"To E—C—"—"for he had seen similar titles in the collected poems of Lord Byron,"[7] and he is following Wordsworth's famous description of poetry and the poet by recollecting in tranquillity the "experience" he himself has had alongside the responding emotions of the earlier scene. More: *what* he writes is completely autobiographical and typically lyrical and specifically Romantic—in short, Stephen spiritualizes, de-materializing every object:

> … by dint of brooding on the incident, he thought himself into confidence. During this process all these elements which he deemed common and insignificant fell out of the scene. There remained no trace of the tram itself nor of the tram-men nor of the horses; nor did he and she appear vividly. The verses told only of the night and the balmy breeze and the maiden lustre of the moon. Some undefined sorrow was hidden in the hearts of the protagonists as they stood in silence beneath the leafless trees and when the moment of farewell had come the kiss, which had been withheld by one, was given by both.[8]

The verses thus end in separation. (Stephen the poet, however, returns to his mother's room/"womb," a desire Stephen has variously expressed since the dawning of the Oedipal complex in him at Clonglowes.)

Although we are treated to some verses by Stephen earlier in the final chapter—lacking promise, they have to do with ivy "whin[ing] upon the wall"[9]—it is only toward the end that we are given an apparently complete

DOI: 10.1057/9781137399823.0007

poem. In the complex metrical form of the villanelle, written ten years after the abortive incident on the tram, it perpetuates the Romantic pattern of lyric and poetic autobiography, riddled with religious imagery now employed in secular and carnal fashion, its themes completely reflective of Stephen's innermost and persistent desires—I quote it entire and just as it appears in the novel, in italics:

> *Are you not weary of ardent ways,*
> *Lure of the fallen seraphim?*
> *Tell no more of enchanted days.*
>
> *Your eyes have set man's heart ablaze*
> *And you have had your will of him.*
> *Are you not weary of ardent ways?*
>
> *Above the flame the smoke of praise*
> *Goes up from ocean rim to rim.*
> *Tell no more of enchanted days.*
>
> *Our broken cries and mournful lays*
> *Rise in one eucharistic hymn.*
> *Are you not weary of ardent ways?*
>
> *While sacrificing hands upraise*
> *The chalice flowing to the brim,*
> *Tell no more of enchanted days.*
>
> *And still you hold our longing gaze*
> *With languorous look and lavish limb!*
> *Are you not weary of ardent ways?*
> *Tell no more of enchanted days.*[10]

It is critical that we understand the origin of the verses: Stephen had seen Emma Cleary some time before this writing, and the sight of her again sends him off into paroxysms of desire, frustration, anger, and imagination. He sleeps, eventually, his "soul" said to become—suggestively—"all dewy wet"; then it awakens, and he thinks "The night had been enchanted. In a dream or vision he had known the ecstasy of seraphic life." He begins, then, to compose his verses: "O! In the virgin womb of the imagination the word was made flesh. Gabriel the seraph had come to the virgin's chamber."[11] Soon, however, ecstasy turns to anger and jealousy: "It was like the image of the young priest in whose company he had seen her last, looking at him out of dove's eyes, toying with the pages of his Irish phrasebook."[12] Stephen proceeds to think "he had done well to leave her to flirt with her priest, to toy with a church which was the scullerymaid

DOI: 10.1057/9781137399823.0007

of christendom" (he thinks even less of Protestantism). He then launches
into this internal tirade, which confirms the darkness and evil within him:

> … she was a figure of the womanhood of her country, a batlike soul wak-
> ing to the consciousness of itself in darkness and secrecy and loneliness,
> tarrying awhile, loveless and sinless, with her mild lover and leaving him
> to whisper of innocent transgressions in the latticed ear of a priest. His
> anger against her found vent in coarse railing at her paramour, whose name
> and voice and features offended his baffled pride: a priested peasant, with
> a brother a policeman in Dublin and a brother a potboy in Moycullen. To
> him she would unveil her soul's shy nakedness, to one who was but schooled
> in the discharging of a formal rite rather than to him, a priest of the eternal
> imagination, transmuting the daily bread of experience into the radiant
> body of everlasting life.[13]

Finally, just before we are given the villanelle, with its embrace of the
enchanted and repudiation of "the ardent," Joyce offers this account
of Stephen's consciousness, in which sex and imagination combine in
decidedly unorthodox fashion. Not for the first or the only time, Stephen
literally expresses his love of himself, separate from the presumed object
of desire, and satisfying that desire via the substitute that is himself and
his imagination:

> A glow of desire kindled again his soul and fired and fulfilled all his body.
> Conscious of his desire she was waking from odorous sleep, the temptress
> of his villanelle. Her eyes, dark and with a look of languor, were opening to
> his eyes. Her nakedness yielded to him, radiant, warm, odorous and lavish-
> limbed, enfolded him like a shining cloud, enfolded him like water with a
> liquid life: and like a cloud of vapour or like waters circumfluent in space
> the liquid letters of speech, symbols of the element of mystery flowed forth
> from his brain.[14]

Stephen's spiritualizations thus produce the very materializations that he
would rise above. Separate from others and utterly alone, he imagines
himself happy, needing no one else.

Aesthetics mirrors poetics, both of them *forged* in the "smithy" of
Stephen's desire for an asceticism that realizes itself only in its apparent opposite. Stephen's "purity perplex"—shared, incidentally, with
another Romantic, the American Transcendentalist Henry David
Thoreau—remains undeterred and ever-present in the pattern we have
been observing. The issue is not (just) the nature of the theory (that
Stephen cobbles together from a number of sources, prominently including Aristotle and Aquinas) but the *use* to which he puts it and for which

DOI: 10.1057/9781137399823.0007

he formulates it, a fact that complicates if it does not actually undercut the theory as stated.

The final chapter of *A Portrait* centers on Stephen's aesthetics as presented to his friends, including the irrepressible Lynch (a sort of Horatio to Stephen's Hamlet). Joyce here represents Stephen's conversation, but Stephen's discourse is more a lecture, for he is barely aware of another's presence, barely aware of a particular auditor and impersonal, befitting the nature of his aesthetics. Stephen thus begins, his pride on full display: "Aristotle has not defined pity and terror. I have." The down-to-earth Lynch interposes that he is sick from having been out drinking the night before, but Stephen is oblivious, continuing:

> —Pity is the feeling which arrests the mind in the presence of whatever is grave and constant in human sufferings and unites it with the human sufferer. Terror is the feeling which arrests the mind in the presence of whatsoever is grave and constant in human sufferings and unites it with the secret cause.[15]

This is more like written discourse than oral, and on display in it is a matching emphasis on the "arrest" of mind and emotions, in perfect keeping with Stephen's desire to transcend the messy and inescapable facts of the human condition. Following Lynch's request that Stephen "repeat," he responds, including with this elaboration, which affirms his desire to transcend desire and to find a state of "arrest," absent such "ardent ways" as his own verses also repudiate:

> —The tragic emotion, in fact, is a face looking two ways, towards terror and towards pity, both of which are phases of it. You see I use the word *arrest*. I mean that the tragic emotion is static. Or rather the dramatic emotion is. The feelings excited by improper art are kinetic, desire of loathing. Desire urges us to possess, to go to something; loathing urges us to abandon, to go from something. These are kinetic emotions. The arts which excite them, pornographical or didactic, are therefore improper arts. The esthetic emotion (I use the general term) is therefore static. The mind is arrested and raised above desire and loathing.[16]

To be sure, this promulgation of aesthetic theory offers a refinement of Stephen's general loathing of most things physical. It is, then, a modified transcendence of his previous oscillations between (sexual) desire and (physical) loathing, which had led him to see women as either Marian figures (his mother's name is also Mary) or whores, such as those to whom he turns (as mother-substitutes). In his aesthetic theory, he thus reaches a

DOI: 10.1057/9781137399823.0007

stasis, a sort of middle position that *is* stasis itself (and "arrest"), avoiding emotion altogether, becoming a kind of automaton, such as he appears in these so-called conversations with "friends." This position differs, obviously, from Eliot's "impossible union" of caring and not-caring: Stephen's starting-point is not caring but its very (would-be) transcendence.

Stephen proceeds to the perhaps-surprising acknowledgment that "we are all animals. I also am an animal." As always, he goes on, in the event re-confirming the autobiographical origin of his theories:

> —But we are just now in a mental world, Stephen continued. The desire and loathing excited by improper esthetic means are really unesthetic emotions not only because they are kinetic in character but also because they are not more than physical. Our flesh shrinks from what it dreads and responds to the stimulus of what it desires by a purely reflex action of the nervous system. Our eyelid closes before we are aware that the fly is about to enter our eye.[17]

To this possible echo of Swift's satire on dehumanization, Lynch responds "critically": "Not always." Without missing a beat, Stephen proceeds, his voice that of (distanced—and safe) writing, not speaking:

> —In the same way, said Stephen, your flesh responded to the stimulus of a naked statue but it was, I say, simply a reflex action of the nerves. Beauty expressed by the artist cannot awaken in us an emotion which is kinetic or a sensation which is purely physical. It awakens, or ought to awaken, or induces, or ought to induce, an esthetic stasis, an ideal pity or an ideal terror, a stasis called forth, prolonged, and at last dissolved by what I call the rhythm of beauty.

With the explicit reference to the "ideal," any cat left in the bag springs forth.[18]

Meanwhile, Lynch continues with banter, unreciprocated, of course. After asking for definitions of both rhythm and beauty, he reminds Stephen that "though I did eat a cake of cowdung once, I admire only beauty."[19] He is as earth-bound as Stephen is airy (and Laputan). Raising his cap, "blushing slightly," and laying "his hand on Lynch's thick tweed sleeve," this last a reminder of the concrete and the physical that Stephen generally avoids, thus clinging to aesthetics while those all about him are engaging in political discussions and sometimes commitments of time, self, and effort, he says:

> —We are right, and the others are wrong. To speak of these things and to try to understand their nature and, having understood it, to try slowly and *humbly* and constantly to express, to press out again, from the *gross*

DOI: 10.1057/9781137399823.0007

earth or what it brings forth, from sound and shape and colour which are the prison gates of our soul, an image of the beauty we have come to understand—that is art. (Italics added)[20]

Lynch still wants to know what art is, which Stephen now defines as "the human disposition of sensible or intelligible matter for an esthetic end." It does not omit or violate the true. Like beauty, in fact, according to Stephen, "the true produces also a stasis of the mind." He tells Lynch: "You would not write your name in pencil across the hypothenuse of a right-angled triangle." No, says Lynch: "give me the hypothenuse of the Venus of Praxiteles."[21] Stephen then goes on, again undeterred:

> —Static therefore…Plato, I believe, said that beauty is the splendour of truth. I don't think that it has a meaning but the true and the beautiful are akin. Truth is beheld by the intellect which is appeased by the most satisfying relations of the sensible. The first step in the direction of truth is to understand the frame and scope of the intellect itself, to comprehend the act itself of intellection. Aristotle's entire system of philosophy rests upon his psychology and that, I think, rests upon his book of psychology and that, I think, rests on his statement that the same attribute cannot at the same time belong to and not belong to the same subject. The first step in the direction of beauty is to understand the frame and scope of the imagination, to comprehend the act itself of esthetic apprehension.

With the statement denying the simultaneity of "attributes" belonging to different "subjects," another cat flies from the bag. "Arrest" stands opposed to (Incarnational) "attend."

Lynch persists, asking again for a definition, this time "impatiently," "But what is beauty? Out with another definition. Something we see and like! Is that the best you and Aquinas can do?" Stephen then begins again: "Let us take woman," to which Lynch replies "fervently," "Let us take her!" Stephen follows in yet another essential monologue, his separation from common humanity, partly represented by Lynch, at least as thoroughgoing as Lemuel Gulliver's.

> —The Greek, the Turk, the Chinese, the Copt, the Hottentot, said Stephen, all admire a different type of female beauty. That seems to be a *maze* out of which we cannot escape. I see however two ways out. One is this hypothesis: that every physical quality admired by men in women is in direct connection with the manifold functions of women for the propagation of the species. It may be so. The world, it seems, is *drearier* than even you, Lynch, imagined. For my part I dislike that way out. It leads to eugenics rather than to esthetic. (Italics added)[22]

DOI: 10.1057/9781137399823.0007

The word "maze," of course, is an ironic reference to that structure from
which the mythical figure Dedalus had to free the minotaur; that Stephen
utters the word and then "flies by" it indicates the blown possibility
of recognizing an "attended" point. He continues on in true pedantic,
clinical, and insouciant fashion. The "other way out," Stephen explains,
is that

> though the same object may not seem beautiful to all people, all people who
> admire a beautiful object find in it certain relations which satisfy and coin-
> cide with the stages themselves of all esthetic apprehension. These relations
> of the sensible, visible to you through one form and to me through another,
> must be therefore the necessary qualities of beauty.[23]

Some back-and-forth regarding Aquinas follows, and then they are met
by another student, named Donovan, who, among other things, men-
tions Goethe, Lessing, and the *Laocoon*. In a bit, after Donovan's depar-
ture, Stephen starts up again, not having lost the thread of his discourse:

> —To finish what I was saying about beauty, the most satisfying relations of
> the sensible must therefore correspond to the necessary phases of artistic
> apprehension. Find these and you find the qualities of universal beauty.
> Aquinas says: *ad pulcritudinem tria requiruntur, integritas, consonantia, clari-
> tas.* I translate it so: *Three things are needed for beauty, wholeness, harmony
> and radiance.*[24]

Noticing a butcher boy's basket, Stephen directs Lynch's attention to it,
revealing the separatist basis of Stephen's intellectual apprehension:

> In order to see that basket, said Stephen, your mind first of all separates
> the basket from the rest of the visible universe which is not the basket. The
> first phase of apprehension is a bounding line drawn about the object to be
> apprehended. An esthetic image is presented to us either in space or in time.
> What is audible is presented in time, what is visible is presented in space.
> But, temporal or spatial, the esthetic image is first luminously apprehended
> as selfbounded and selfcontained upon the immeasurable background of
> space or time which is not it. You apprehended it as *one* thing. You see it as
> one whole. You apprehended its wholeness. That is *integritas.*[25]

Art is, then, a thing apart, separated and intact; it can be connected with
nothing besides itself. Like the ascetically inclined speaker early in Eliot's
Ash-Wednesday: Six Poems, Stephen assumes that "what is actual" is so
only for one time and one place.[26]

    With evident satisfaction, Stephen moves on to the second of the
three phases of apprehension. In all of this, Joyce reveals, by means of

DOI: 10.1057/9781137399823.0007

his character's discourse on aesthetics, his essential way of responding, in the process adding yet another instance of the pattern ubiquitous and determinative for Stephen. It may well be, of course, that Stephen's theory captures the heart of intellectual apprehension.

—Then, said Stephen, you pass from point to point, led by its formal lines; you apprehend it as balanced part against part within its limits; you feel the rhythm of its structure. In other words the synthesis of immediate perception is followed by the analysis of apprehension. Having first felt that it is *one* thing you feel now that it is a *thing*. You apprehend it as complex, multiple, divisible, separable, made up of its parts, the result of its parts and their sum, harmonious. That is *consonantia*.[27]

"Bull's eye again," responds Lynch. "Tell me now what is *claritas* and you win the cigar."[28]

Stephen is, of course, all too willing to oblige, and so moves immediately to the third and final phase of apprehension. Regarding *claritas*, he claims that "the connotation of the word,"

is rather vague. Aquinas uses a term which seems to be inexact. It baffled me for a long time. It would lead you to believe that he had in mind symbolism or idealism, the supreme quality of beauty being a light from some other world, the idea of which the matter is but the shadow, the reality of which it is but the symbol.[29]

Here we recall, or should recall, that Stephen later, pointedly, misremembers a line in the Renaissance prose writer Thomas Nashe as "*Darkness falls from the air*" when it is, in fact, "*Brightness falls from the air*,"[30] an error that captures exactly Stephen's view of the world. As to Aquinas, in any case, Stephen says,

I thought he might mean that *claritas* is the artistic discovery and representation of the divine purpose in anything or a force of generalisation which would make the esthetic image a universal one, make it outshine its proper conditions. But that is literary talk. I understand it so. When you have apprehended that basket as one thing and have then analysed it according to its form and apprehended it as a thing you make the only synthesis which is logically and esthetically permissible. You see that it is that thing which it is and no other thing. The radiance of which he speaks is the scholastic *quidditas*, the *whatness* of a thing. This supreme quality is felt by the artist when the esthetic image is first conceived in his imagination. The mind in that mysterious instant Shelley likened beautifully to a fading coal. The instant wherein that supreme quality of beauty, the clear radiance of the esthetic image, is apprehended luminously by the mind which has been arrested by

DOI: 10.1057/9781137399823.0007

its wholeness and fascinated by its harmony is the luminous silent stasis of esthetic pleasure, a spiritual state very like to that cardiac condition which the Italian physiologist Luigi Galvani, using a phrase almost as beautiful as Shelley's, called the enchantment of the heart."[31]

In *The Sacred Wood*, Eliot for one roundly rejects the notion that the poet "endeavours to produce in us a *state*."[32]

Following this long, uninterrupted holding-forth, Stephen pauses, feeling that "his words had called up around them a thoughtenchanted silence."[33] He frequently, and suggestively, imagines something surrounding him, most often something fluid and even lambent; Stephen also likes to imagine enchantment. Here in particular, he is creative of that which he desires. Lemuel Gulliver, as we have seen, engages in something both similar and different: he adapts, specifically to the extra-ordinary that he always encounters in his travels. In both his case and Stephen's—to refer again to Eliot's point regarding Romanticism in *The Sacred Wood* (i.e., it is a short-cut to the strangeness without the reality)—reality is bypassed and transcended.[34] Neither Stephen Dedalus, who seeks escape from "the gross earth," nor Lemuel Gulliver, ever-curious, ever-credulous, and satisfied only when away from home, preferably on an island floating above constraining and "gross" and "sluggish" earth, finds the extra-ordinary in the ordinary and familiar.

In his "conversation" with Lynch, Stephen begins again, clarifying, elaborating, and moving toward a final, critical statement regarding literature, to which he will pledge and commit his life:

> —What I have said refers to beauty in the wider sense of the word, in the sense which the word has in the literary tradition. In the marketplace it has another sense. When we speak of beauty in the second sense of the term our judgment is influenced in the first place by the art itself and by the form of that art. The image, it is clear, must be set between the mind or senses of the artist himself and the mind or senses of others. If you bear this in memory you will see that art necessarily divides itself into three forms progressing from one to the next. These forms are: the lyrical form, the form wherein the artist presents his image in immediate relation to himself; the epical form, the form wherein he presents his image in mediate relation to himself and to others; the dramatic form, the form wherein he presents his image in immediate relation to others.[35]

I for one doubt any sort of "progress" in art, but however that may be, Stephen's procedure is clear enough: he imagines a progress from closeness to distance, the artist removing his "image" ever farther away from

DOI: 10.1057/9781137399823.0007

himself—and ever-closer "to others." Irony now piles upon irony: so close to himself, Stephen is (forever) separate from others, although he claims his art will be just the opposite.

Finally, Stephen offers, as a sort of *Summa*, Aquinas's well-known account of just this point of view, with the artist as transcendent being, indifferent and uninvolved, absolutely "other," in other words. The passage, full of judgment and bias (and arrogance), seems to rhyme even so with Eliot's account, a few years later, of the poet's necessary "surrender" of his "personality."[36] Stephen's account is based in speculation:

—Lessing, said Stephen, should not have taken a group of statues to write of. The art, being inferior, does not present the forms I spoke of distinguished clearly one from another. Even in literature, the highest and most spiritual art, the forms are often confused. The lyrical is in fact the simplest verbal vesture of an instant of emotion, a rhythmical cry such as ages ago cheered on the man who pulled at the oar or dragged stones up a slope. He who utters it is more conscious of the instant of emotion than of himself as feeling emotion. The simplest epical form is seen emerging out of lyrical literature when the artist prolongs and broods upon himself as the centre of an epical event and this form progresses till the centre of emotional gravity is equidistant from the artist himself and from others. The narrative is no longer purely personal. The personality of the artist passes into the narration itself, flowing round and round the persons and the action like a vital sea. This progress you will see easily in that old English ballad *Turpin Hero* which begins in the first person and ends in the third person.[37]

The reader cannot help but apply Stephen's words here to Joyce's procedure in *A Portrait*: that the novel ends in and with his protagonist's diary points to a distance between the two while affirming Stephen's separation from others—and his author's from him. In the passage we are just now reading, Stephen turns to the completion of "progress," re-turning to the reiterated image of being surrounded by liquid satisfactions, an image that surely connotes the womb, the ultimate object of Stephen's desire, after all, and the paradigm of the escape that his artistic theory and his poetic practice represent. Stephen's words describing aesthetics mirror exactly his desire as we have seen it embodied throughout *A Portrait*:

The dramatic form is reached when the vitality which has flowed and eddied round each person fills every person with such vital force that he or she assumes a proper and intangible esthetic life. The personality of the artist, at first a cry or a cadence or a mood and then a fluid and lambent narrative, finally refines itself out of existence, impersonalises itself, so to speak.

DOI: 10.1057/9781137399823.0007

> The esthetic image in the dramatic form is life purified in and reprojected from the human imagination. The mystery of esthetic like that of material creation is accomplished. The artist, like the God of the creation, remains within or behind or beyond or above his handiwork, invisible, refined out of existence, indifferent, paring his fingernails.

Lynch's response is critical and devastating, encapsulating Joyce's satirical thesis throughout the novel: "Trying to refine them ['his fingernails'] also out of existence."[38]

Joyce's extended treatment of Stephen's aesthetics in the fifth and final chapter, detailed and precise (if not also pedantic), turns out to be a major rhetorical device. Essentially a series of mini-lectures, Stephen's "speeches" occur in the presence of "friends," particularly the irrepressible (and deconstructing) Lynch. They may also be seen as *dramatic monologues*, for Stephen's words betray him, at least to the reader (if not also to comically mundane but Socratically acute Lynch, who on occasion is seen as *lynch*-ing his friend). Stephen's words, in fact, show us that he is in the process of violating his own aesthetic principles, for his theory is itself far from being disinterested; it is, instead, built on the foundation of escape from human involvement and engagement that Stephen everywhere seeks. The so-called objective theory that Stephen promulgates, and that Lynch slyly deconstructs, flounders on its own impossibility to meet Stephen's needs.

Eliot's striking, anti-Romantic account of the poet and the making of poetry occurs in "Tradition and the Individual Talent," included in *The Sacred Wood: Essays on Poetry and Criticism* (1920). The whole essay bears on our questions and Stephen's seemingly apposite argument regarding the artist's invisibility (his preferred term "art," to "literature" or "poetry," signals both his aggrandizing penchant and his sense of self-importance), but the following paragraph pinpoints the issues at stake.

Eliot has used the analogy of the catalyst to describe the creative process involved. Immediately, I sense this difference: Stephen knows something of the aesthetic theories of Aristotle and Aquinas, Eliot probably knows them (and much more philosophy) too, but he also knows people. He points as well to the complexity of emotion involved in poetry, whereas Stephen is all about his own revulsion at the prospect of things material and especially those of "the gross earth." In addition, Eliot signals the difference between art and life; Stephen would remake life in art's image. Stephen, I suspect, would never deign to use the word "business" to name the work of the poet.

DOI: 10.1057/9781137399823.0007

It is not in his personal emotions, the emotions provoked by particular events in his life, that the poet is in any way remarkable or interesting. His particular emotions may be simple, or crude, or flat. The emotion in his poetry will be a very complex thing, but not with the complexity of the emotions of people who have very complex or unusual emotions in life. One error, in fact, of eccentricity in poetry is to seek for new human emotions to express; and in this search for novelty in the wrong place it discovers the perverse. The business of the poet is not to find new emotions, but to use the ordinary ones and, in working them up into poetry, to express feelings which are not in actual emotions at all. And emotions which he has never experienced will serve his turn as well as those familiar to him.[39]

Eliot thus stays with the ordinary (emotions), the poet's "business" being to make "new" poetry out of them (a parallel to the issue of "tradition" and "the individual," the temporal and the timeless). In the event, Eliot would have the poet serve the poetry, but Stephen would have the poetry serve his private needs. Stephen Dedalus is Wordsworth's Romantic poet materialized.

In "Tradition and the Individual Talent," Eliot continues, directly taking on Wordsworth's then-revolutionary definition of poetry:

Consequently, we must believe that "emotion recollected in tranquillity" is an inexact formula. For it is neither emotion, nor recollection, nor, without distortion of meaning, tranquillity. It is a concentration, and a new thing resulting from the concentration, of a very great number of experiences which to the practical and active person would not seem to be experiences at all; it is a concentration which does not happen consciously or of deliberation. These experiences are not "recollected," and they finally unite in an atmosphere which is "tranquil" only in that it is a passive attending upon the event.[40]

No hint here of the "arrest" toward which Stephen so readily inclines. Eliot then proceeds to conclude the paragraph:

Of course this is not quite the whole story. There is a great deal, in the writing of poetry, which must be conscious and deliberate. In fact, the bad poet is usually unconscious where he ought to be conscious, and conscious where he ought to be unconscious. Both errors tend to make him "personal." Poetry is not a turning loose of emotion, but an escape from emotion; it is not the expression of personality, but an escape from personality. But, of course, only those who have personality and emotions know what it means to want to escape from these things.[41]

DOI: 10.1057/9781137399823.0007

Believing art and life to be different, Eliot thus offers *poetry* as an "escape from emotion" and with it from the "personality" of the poet; Stephen, though, seeks an escape from emotion through an art that is itself emotion-less. Eliot's poetry is highly emotional, Stephen's hardly so. Eliot's personality finds no place in the poetry, whereas Stephen's is everywhere present, if most so precisely in its quest of impersonality. Thus as Stephen says to Lynch at one telling point, "The personality of the artist passes into the narration itself."[42]

In the final analysis, we surely have to conclude, Stephen's aesthetic, and the art he plans to make, is both personal and impersonal. That is so because the impersonal is determined by the personal, chosen and striving for personal ends, those of his own autobiographical needs and desires. Those needs and desires constitute the movement of the pattern that is everywhere present and functional in Stephen Dedalus's life, giving to it whatever meaning it has.

Notes

1   Jonathan Swift, *"Gulliver's Travels" and Other Writings*, ed. Louis A. Landa (Boston, MA: Riverside-Houghton Mifflin, 1960), 133.
2   James Joyce, *A Portrait of the Artist as a Young Man*, 1916 (New York: Viking-Penguin, 1964), 169.
3   Ibid., 172.
4   Swift, 331.
5   Joyce, 253.
6   Ibid., 71.
7   Ibid., 70.
8   Ibid., 70–71.
9   Ibid., 179.
10   Ibid., 223.
11   Ibid., 217.
12   Ibid., 220.
13   Ibid., 221.
14   Ibid., 223.
15   Ibid., 204.
16   Ibid., 205.
17   Ibid., 206.
18   Ibid.
19   Ibid.

DOI: 10.1057/9781137399823.0007

20 Ibid.
21 Ibid., 207–8.
22 Ibid., 208.
23 Ibid.
24 Ibid., 209.
25 Ibid., 211–12.
26 T.S. Eliot, *Ash-Wednesday: Six Poems* (New York: Putnam, 1930).
27 Ibid.
28 Ibid.
29 Ibid., 212–13.
30 Ibid., 232, 234.
31 Ibid., 213.
32 T.S. Eliot. *The Sacred Wood: Essays on Poetry and Criticism* (London: Methuen, 1920), 145.
33 Joyce, 213,
34 Eliot, *The Sacred Wood*, 28.
35 Joyce, 213–14.
36 Eliot, *The Sacred Wood,* 47.
37 Ibid., 214–15.
38 Ibid., 215.
39 Ibid., 51–52.
40 Ibid., 52.
41 Ibid., 52–53.
42 Joyce, 215.

DOI: 10.1057/9781137399823.0007

6

It's All about Caring and Not-Caring at the Same Time: Or, Home Is Where You Start From

Abstract: *Lemuel Gulliver and Stephen Dedalus are more similar than they would appear. Importantly, neither respects home, both fleeing from it, for a world elsewhere. Gulliver, of course, always starts from his home at Redriff, using it primarily as a launch-site, and shows up again and again, after satisfying his lust to travel and to gain new knowledge, straining for the extra-ordinary in the strange and unfamiliar, never really at home. Stephen flies away, from Ireland to Paris at novel's end, happily leaving family and friends behind, sadly mistaken in believing that separation from home leads to vaunted transcendence—his world remaining dark.*

Atkins, G. Douglas. *Swift, Joyce, and the Flight from Home: Quests of Transcendence and the Sin of Separation*. New York: Palgrave Macmillan, 2014. DOI: 10.1057/9781137399823.0008.

DOI: 10.1057/9781137399823.0008

God loves from Whole to Parts: but human soul
Must rise from Individual to the Whole.
Self-love but serves the virtuous mind to wake,
As the small pebble stirs the peaceful lake;
The centre mov'd, a circle strait succeeds,
Another still, and still another spreads,
Friend, parent, neighbour, first it will embrace,
His country next, and next all human race,
Wide and more wide, th'o'erflowings of the mind
Take ev'ry creature in, of ev'ry kind;
Earth smiles around, with boundless bounty blest,
And Heav'n beholds its image in his breast.

Alexander Pope, *An Essay on Man*

i.

Gulliver would seem to have this much right, at least compared with Stephen Dedalus: he starts from his geographical home (as well as returns there). In a grand gesture, Stephen flees from his home, in the process escaping not just from his mother-country but also from his mother-church and his biological mother (who just may be the ultimate object of his desire). Both Stephen and Gulliver begin with abundance of self-love, but neither one of them moves beyond it—one thing from which they do not separate.

As we have seen, time and again, Gulliver leaves home, essentially forgets about it (and its inhabitants, his wife and increasing number of children), on occasion expresses the hope never to return there (the Flying or Floating Island, Laputa, being "the most delicious spot of ground on the earth").[1] If anything, Stephen is more determined, even less attached, planning to "fly by those nets" of "nationality, language, religion": to Davin's statement that "a man's country comes first," Stephen offers his famous definition of Ireland as "the old sow that eats her farrow."[2] He would escape totally, absolutely.

For Gulliver, with his "violent" desire of knowledge and the new, home is (merely) a launch-site. It remains nothing more, even after his final voyage, for as he makes clear in his letter from Redriff to his cousin Sympson, he had immediately set about (in his exalted terms) reforming humankind, removing "all tincture" of vice and corruption,

DOI: 10.1057/9781137399823.0008

and fully expecting in a matter of six or seven months to have accomplished nothing else. However, having learned that "my book hath [not] produced one single effect according to mine intentions," he regrets attempting "so absurd a project as reforming the yahoo race in this kingdom." Ever the self-satisfied, curious, and credulous, he writes these parting words: "I have done with all such visionary schemes for ever."[3] The words are, of course, allusive and highly charged. They embody a final separation.

Stephen reaches no such "stasis" at the end of *A Portrait of the Artist as a Young Man.* On the contrary, he remains as will ful as ever, having vowed, Satanically, "*Non serviam*" (I will not serve).[4] Behind him, like Swift behind Gulliver, very much engaged, rather than transcendent or invisible (thus different from Stephen's "artist"), Joyce employs innocent-looking words much as he does the "mythical method" that Eliot celebrated and embraced.[5] In the penultimate diary entry, that narrative mode fully revealing the author's distance from his protagonist, Joyce charges the key word "forge" with ironic meaning, thanks in part to his use of the word twice before in the novel.

> Welcome, O life! I go to encounter for the millionth time the reality of experience and to *forge* in the smithy of my soul the uncreated conscience of my race. (italics added)[6]

Every word lies: *Splendide mendax.*[7]

Gulliver never really "returns" to home and family; he merely shows up, at least once having planted his seed (which grows, no thanks to him), and then leaves again, shortly. Back in Redriff for the final time, he does not—for once—adjust, attempting to remake family, people, and place in Houyhnhnm-image. By no stretch of the imagination does he "arrive where [he] started/ And know the place for the first time" (Eliot, "Little Gidding," *Four Quartets*).[8] For him, home, and beginning, do not stand as standards of measurement in rendered comparisons with the horses. Inattentive, Gulliver has no home to attend (him).

Accordingly, he has to seek, perchance to find, the extra-ordinary in the strange and unfamiliar. There is nothing of much importance to him in what he knows. In this way, he is a Romantic. As Eliot said, in a passage we have seen more than once before:

> …the only cure for Romanticism is to analyse it. What is permanent and good in Romanticism is curiosity, a curiosity which recognizes that any life, if accurately and profoundly penetrated, is interesting and always strange.

DOI: 10.1057/9781137399823.0008

Romanticism is a short cut to the strangeness without the reality, and it
leads its disciples only back upon themselves.[9]

Lemuel Gulliver is closely—and remarkably—attended by these words
of Eliot in *The Sacred Wood*.

ii.

In a poem known as "elusive," the following verse at the close of *Ash-
Wednesday: Six Poems* is one of the most enigmatic—I include the preced-
ing line as well: "Suffer us not to mock ourselves with falsehood/ Suffer
us to care and not to care."[10]

Our usual temptation, it seems, is to assume that Eliot has in mind a
transcendence of these apparent opposites, if not a synthesis of thesis
and antithesis. But that is not what he means—nor is it the way satire
works.

Eliot literally means the capacity to hold both caring and not-caring in
mind and heart simultaneously. At first glance, that seems impossible—
but then Incarnation made possible precisely that joining, being the
paradigmatic instance of "impossible union." How, though, is it possible
for the ordinary human—not a "saint"—to do anything like this?

You (always) start from home. But unlike with Lemuel Gulliver, for
one, and Stephen Dedalus, for another, "home" means *caring*. You pro-
ceed in, through, and by means of it.

In "Little Gidding," as he moves toward closing *Four Quartets*, Eliot
turns to the matter of "three conditions" that "often look alike/ Yet differ
completely."[11] One is attachment to self, things, and persons; another is
detachment from self, things, and persons; and, "growing between them"
is indifference, "Which resembles the others as death resembles life." To
be indifferent is to be (merely) dying, as *The Waste Land* amply represents. In praying to care and not to care at the same time, the speaker in
Ash-Wednesday most certainly is not seeking indifference. What follows
in "Little Gidding" offers (at least) a hint how that "impossible union"
works:

> This is the use of memory:
> For liberation—not less of love but expanding
> Of love beyond desire, and so liberation
> From the future as well as the past.[12]

DOI: 10.1057/9781137399823.0008

That Eliot has in mind the necessity of beginning from love, as from caring, is confirmed by the verses immediately following that declare, explaining, that in the same fashion "love of a country/ Begins as attachment to our own field of action" and then moves outward, beyond. In other words, you begin—at home—with attachment, but your work is far from done. You go in, through, and by means of attachment, caring, and home—not to detachment, let alone indifference—but to a union, albeit seemingly impossible, of such closeness to an equally necessary distance.

Both are necessary. To settle for one, without the other, is to rest in half-truth, that is, in "falsehood." Memory and desire are "stirred" at the outset of *The Waste Land*, and Stephen's desire certainly drives his quest of the impersonal and the transcendental, in a sense deconstructing it. Memory looks, longingly, backwards, toward the past; desire looks, longingly, forward, toward the future. Incarnation is the intersection of the timeless with time, of transcendence with immanence, from which it is inseparable.

To say it again, in other words: Caring equals desiring, not necessarily of just a selfish or egoistical sort. Not-caring equals, perhaps surprisingly, that "expanding/ Of love beyond desire." Desire needs not to be purged—purgation being a pagan idea, after all, involving transcendence (alone). Desire needs be refined, purified, a thoroughly Christian notion (that, unlike Gulliver, retains the starting-point in play although it be refined).

Notes

1   Jonathan Swift, *"Gulliver's Travels" and Other Writings*, ed. Louis A. Landa (Boston, MA: Riverside-Houghton Mifflin, 1960), 133.
2   James Joyce, *A Portrait of the Artist as a Young Man*, 1916 (New York: Viking-Penguin, 1964), 203.
3   Swift, 4, 6.
4   Joyce, 239 (see also 117).
5   T.S. Eliot, "Ulysses, Order, and Myth," *Dial* 75 (Nov. 1923), 480–83.
6   Joyce, 253.
7   The phrase appears on the title page of the 1735 edition of *Travels*.
8   T.S. Eliot, *Four Quartets* (New York: Harcourt, Brace, 1943).
9   T.S. Eliot, *The Sacred Wood: Essays on Poetry and Criticism* (London: Methuen, 1920), 27–28.

DOI: 10.1057/9781137399823.0008

10   T.S. Eliot, *Ash-Wednesday: Six Poems* (New York: Putnam, 1930).

11   On this point, see my *Reading T.S. Eliot: "Four Quartets" and the Journey toward Understanding* (New York: Palgrave Macmillan, 2012).

12   Note, by the way, Eliot's expressiveness in mimicking the "expanding/ Of love" by extending the idea to the line following the gerund, also the strategic placement of the word "liberation," one at the beginning of a line, the other at the end of the following—hardly accidentals.

DOI: 10.1057/9781137399823.0008

Bibliography

Abrams, M.H. *Natural Supernaturalism: Tradition and Revolution in Romantic Literature*. New York: Norton, 1971.

Adams, Robert M. "Jonathan Swift, Thomas Swift, and the Authorship of *A Tale of a Tub*." *Modern Philology*, 64 (1967): 198–232.

Anderson, Chester G. Ed. *A Portrait of the Artist as a Young Man*. By James Joyce. 1916. Viking Critical Edition. New York: Viking, 1976.

Atkins, G. Douglas. *The Faith of John Dryden: Continuity and Change*. Lexington: UP of Kentucky, 1980.

_____ *On the Familiar Essay: Challenging Academic Orthodoxies*. New York: Palgrave Macmillan, 2009.

_____ *Reading Essays: An Invitation*. Athens: U of Georgia P, 2008.

_____ *Swift's Satires on Modernism: Battlegrounds of Reading and Writing*. New York: Palgrave Macmillan, 2013.

_____ *Tracing the Essay: Through Experience to Meaning*. Athens: U of Georgia P, 2005.

Attridge, Derek. Ed. *The Cambridge Companion to James Joyce*. 2nd edn. Cambridge: Cambridge UP, 2004.

Booth, Wayne C. *The Rhetoric of Fiction*. Chicago, IL: U of Chicago P, 1961.

Chesterton, G.K. "A Piece of Chalk." In Philip Lopate, ed., *The Art of the Personal Essay*. New York: Anchor-Doubleday, 1996, 249–52.

Clark, John. *Form and Frenzy in Swift's Tale of a Tub*. Ithaca, NY: Cornell UP, 1970.

DOI: 10.1057/9781137399823.0009

Clifford, James. "Gulliver's Final Voyage: 'Hard' and 'Soft' Schools of Interpretation." In Larry Champion, ed., *Quick Springs of Sense: Studies in the Eighteenth Century.* Athens: U of Georgia P, 1974, 33–49.

Davie, Donald. *These the Companions: Recollections.* Cambridge: Cambridge UP, 1982.

Davis, Walter A. *The Act of Interpretation: A Critique of Literary Reason.* Chicago, IL: U of Chicago P, 1978.

Derrida, Jacques. "Living On: Border Lines." In Harold Bloom, Paul de Man, Jacques Derrida, Geoffrey Hartman, and J. Hillis Miller, eds, *Deconstruction and Criticism.* New York: Seabury P, 1979.

Dryden, John. *Poems and Fables.* Ed. James Kinsley. London: Oxford UP, 1962.

_____ *Religio Laici or A Layman's Faith.* 2nd edn. London, 1683.

_____ *Works* (California Edition): *Poems 1681–1684.* Ed. H.T. Swedenberg, Jr. Berkeley: U of California P, 1972.

Ehrenpreis, Irvin. *Swift: The Man, His Works, and the Age.* Vol. 2 (*Dr. Swift*). Cambridge, MA: Harvard UP, 1969.

Eliot, T.S. *Ash-Wednesday: Six Poems.* New York: Putnam 1930.

_____ *Burnt Norton.* London: Faber and Faber, 1941.

_____ *Collected Poems 1909–1935.* London: Faber and Faber, 1936.

_____ *The Dry Salvages.* London: Faber and Faber, 1941.

_____ *Essays Ancient and Modern.* London: Faber and Faber, 1936.

_____ *For Lancelot Andrewes: Essays on Style and Order.* London: Faber and Gwyer, 1928.

_____ *Four Quartets.* New York: Harcourt, Brace, 1943.

_____ *Little Gidding.* London: Faber and Faber, 1942.

_____ *The Sacred Wood: Essays on Poetry and Criticism.* London: Methuen, 1920.

_____ *Selected Essays.* 3rd edn. London: Faber and Faber, 1951.

_____ *The Use of Poetry and the Use of Criticism.* London: Faber and Faber, 1933.

_____ *The Waste Land.* New York: Boni and Liveright, 1922.

Fakundiny, Lydia. Ed. *The Art of the Essay.* Boston, MA: Houghton Mifflin, 1991.

Fitzgerald, F. Scott. *The Crack-Up.* Ed. Edmund Wilson. New York: New Directions, 1945.

Fox, Christopher. Ed. *The Cambridge Companion to Jonathan Swift.* Cambridge: Cambridge UP, 2003.

DOI: 10.1057/9781137399823.0009

Greene, Donald. *The Age of Exuberance: Backgrounds to Eighteenth Century English Literature.* New York: Random House, 1970.

Hartman, Geoffrey H. *Criticism in the Wilderness: The Study of Literature Today.* New Haven, CT: Yale UP, 1980.

———. *Saving the Text: Literature/Derrida/Philosophy.* Baltimore, MD: Johns Hopkins UP, 1981.

Hill, Christopher. *The World Turned Upside Down: Radical Ideas During the English Revolution.* New York: Viking, 1972.

Hill, Geoffrey. *The Mystery of the Charity of Charles Péguy.* London: Andre Deutsch, 1983.

Jacob, Margaret C. *The Newtonians and the English Revolution, 1689–1720.* Ithaca, NY: Cornell UP, 1976.

Johnson, Samuel. *The Tale of Rasselas, Prince of Abissinia.* 1749. New York: Oxford UP, 2009.

Joyce, James. *A Portrait of the Artist as a Young Man.* 1916. New York: Viking-Penguin, 1976.

———. *A Portrait of the Artist as a Young Man.* The Norton Critical Edition. Ed. John Paul Riquelme. New York: Norton, 2007.

Kenner, Hugh. *Gnomon: Essays on Contemporary Literature.* New York: McDowell, Obolensky, 1958.

———. *The Invisible Poet: T.S. Eliot.* New York: McDowell, Obolensky, 1959.

Kiberd, Declan. *"Ulysses" and Us: The Art of Everyday Life in Joyce's Masterpiece.* New York: Norton, 2009.

Lockerd, Martin. Review of my *T.S. Eliot and the Essay: From "The Sacred Wood" to "Four Quartets." Time Present: The Newsletter of the T.S. Eliot Society,* 77 (Summer 2012), 5–6.

Lytle, Andrew. *The Hero with the Private Parts.* Baton Rouge: Louisiana State UP, 1966.

Mack, Maynard. "Introduction." The Twickenham Edition of *The Poems of Alexander Pope: An Essay on Man.* New Haven, CT: Yale UP, 1950.

Miner, Earl. Ed. *The Works of John Dryden.* Vol. 3. *Poems 1685–1692.* Berkeley: U of California P, 1970.

Monk, Samuel Holt. "The Pride of Lemuel Gulliver." *Sewanee Review* 63 (1955), 48–71.

Murry, J. Middleton. *Jonathan Swift: A Critical Biography.* London: Jonathan Cape, 1954.

DOI: 10.1057/9781137399823.0009

Norris, Margot. *Virgin and Veteran Readings of "Ulysses."* New York: Palgrave Macmillan, 2011.

O'Connor, Flannery. *Mystery and Manners.* Ed. Sally and Robert Fitzgerald. New York: Farrar, Straus and Giroux, 1970.

Paulson, Ronald. *Theme and Structure in Swift's "A Tale of a Tub."* New Haven, CT: Yale UP, 1960.

Pope, Alexander. *Poetry and Prose.* Ed. Aubrey Williams. Boston, MA: Riverside-Houghton Mifflin, 1969.

Price, Martin. *Swift's Rhetorical Art: A Study in Structure and Meaning.* New Haven, CT: Yale UP, 1953.

Rawson, Claude. *God, Gulliver, and Genocide: Barbarism and the European Imagination, 1492–1945.* Oxford: Oxford UP, 2001.

Rosenheim, Edward W. *Swift and the Satirist's Art.* Chicago, IL: U of Chicago P, 1963.

Schneidau, Herbert N. *Sacred Discontent: The Bible and Western Tradition.* Baton Rouge: Louisiana State UP, 1976.

Sisson, C.H. *The Avoidance of Literature: Collected Essays.* Manchester: Carcanet, 1978.

Starkman, Miriam K. *Swift's Satire on Learning in "A Tale of a Tub."* Princeton, NJ: Princeton UP, 1950.

Sutherland, James. *English Satire.* Cambridge: Cambridge UP, 1962.

Swift, Jonathan. *Gulliver's Travels.* The Norton Critical Edition. Ed. Albert J. Rivero. 3rd edn. New York: Norton, 2001.

—— *"Gulliver's Travels" and Other Writings.* Ed. Louis A. Landa. Boston, MA: Riverside-Houghton Mifflin, 1960.

—— *The Mechanical Operation of the Spirit.* In *"A Tale of a Tub" and Other Works.* Ed. Angus Ross and David Woolley. New York: Oxford UP, 2008. 126–41.

—— *The Poems of Jonathan Swift.* Ed. Harold Williams. 2nd edn. Oxford: Clarendon P, 1958. 3 vols.

Thoreau, Henry David. *Walden. In The Portable Thoreau.* Ed. Carl Bode. New York: Viking Penguin, 1947. 258–572.

Thornton, Weldon. *The Antimodernism of Joyce's "A Portrait of the Artist as a Young Man."* Syracuse, NY: Syracuse UP, 1994.

Trinterud, Leonard J. "A.D. 1689: The End of the Clerical World," in *Theology in Sixteenth- and Seventeenth-Century England,* William Andrews Clark Memorial Library Seminar Papers. Los Angeles, CA, 1971.

DOI: 10.1057/9781137399823.0009

Voegelin, Eric. *The New Science of Politics*. Chicago, IL: U of Chicago P, 1952.

Williams, Aubrey. "Introduction." The Twickenham Edition of *The Poems of Alexander Pope: Pastoral Poetry and "An Essay on Criticism."* Ed. Williams. New Haven, CT: Yale UP, 1960.

Williams, Rowan. *Grace and Necessity: Reflections on Art and Love*. Harrisburg, PA: Morehouse, 2005.

Wollaeger, Mark. Ed. *James Joyce's "A Portrait of the Artist as a Young Man": A Casebook*. Oxford UP, 2003.

Wordsworth, William. Preface to *Lyrical Ballads*. In *The Norton Anthology of English Literature*. 6th edn. M.H. Abrams, gen. ed. New York: Norton, 1993. Vol. 2: 141–52.

_____ *The Prelude*. In *The Norton Anthology*. 2 Vols. Vol. 2:207–86.

Wyrick, Deborah. *Jonathan Swift and the Vested Word*. Chapel Hill: U of North Carolina P, 1988.

DOI: 10.1057/9781137399823.0009

Index

DOI: 10.1057/9781137399823.0010

DOI: 10.1057/9781137399823.0010

Lightning Source UK Ltd.
Milton Keynes UK
UKOW04n0514111213

222789UK00002B/2/P